Unfinished Message

A CALIFORNIA LEGACY BOOK

Santa Clara University and Heyday Books are pleased to publish the California Legacy series, vibrant and relevant writings drawn from California's past and present.

Santa Clara University—founded in 1851 on the site of the eighth of California's original 21 missions—is the oldest institution of higher learning in the state. A Jesuit institution, it is particularly aware of its contribution to California's cultural heritage and its responsibility to preserve and celebrate that heritage.

Heyday Books, founded in 1974, specializes in critically acclaimed books on California literature, history, natural history, and ethnic studies.

Books in the California Legacy series will appear as anthologies, single author collections, reprints of important books, and original works. Taken together, these volumes will bring readers a new perspective on California's cultural life, a perspective that honors diversity and finds great pleasure in the eloquence of human expression.

Series editor: Terry Beers

Publisher: Malcolm Margolin

Advisory committee: William Deverell, Michael Duty, Peter Facione, Charles Faulhaben, David Fine, Steven Gilbar, Dana Gioia, Gerald Haslam, Ron Hanson, Robert Hass, Timothy Hodson, Maxine Hong Kingston, James Houston, Jeanne Wakatsuki Houston, Frank LaPena, Ursula LeGuin, Tillie Olsen, Ishmael Reed, Robert Senkewicz, Gary Snyder, Kevin Starr, Richard Walker, Alice Waters, Jennifer Watts, Al Young.

Thanks to the English Department at Santa Clara University and to Regis McKenna for their support of the California Legacy series.

Unfinished Message

Selected Works of Toshio Mori

Introduction by
Lawson Fusao Inada

Foreword by Steven Y. Mori

SANTA CLARA UNIVERSITY • SANTA CLARA
HEYDAY BOOKS • BERKELEY

Library of Congress Cataloging-in-Publication Data

Mori, Toshio, 1910-1980
   Unfinished message : selected works of Toshio Mori / introduction by Lawson Fusao Inada.
            p. cm. — (A California legacy book)
Includes bibliographical references.
   ISBN 1-890771-35-X
   1. California—Social life and customs—Fiction. 2. Japanese Americans—Fiction. I. Inada, Lawson Fusao. II. Title. III. Series.
   PS3563.O87163 A6 2000
   813'.54—dc21

                                                      00-010590

Editing: Patricia Wakida
Cover Design: Rebecca LeGates
Interior Design/Typesetting: Jeannine Gendar
Editorial Assistant: Alison Forns
Printing and Binding: Publishers Press, Salt Lake City, Ut

Orders, inquiries, and correspondence should be addressed to:

Heyday Books
P.O. Box 9145, Berkeley, CA 94709
(510) 549-3564, fax (510) 549-1889
www.heydaybooks.com

Printed in the United States of America
10 9 8 7 6 5 4 3 2 1

Contents

Editor's Note

Unfinished Message: Selected Writings of Toshio Mori, an essential compilation of the work of short-story writer Toshio Mori, reveals his keen understanding of the immigrant Japanese in America before the Second World War, and the influence he has had on California literature.

Unfinished Message includes fifteen remarkable stories selected for their literary quality and historical significance; a previously unpublished novel; letters written by Mori to literary comrade William Saroyan, coinciding with the wartime evacuation of West Coast Japanese Americans; and an interview with Mori that was completed shortly before he died in 1980. This collection also includes original commentary by Lawson Fusao Inada, a third-generation Japanese American, poet, and literary activist who has been at the forefront of the Toshio Mori revival since the early 1970s. His introduction illuminates Mori, the writer, as well as his work.

Some of the stories in *Unfinished Message* appeared originally in periodicals; Mori's work was published in *The Coast, Common Ground, Current Life, Iconograph, Pacific Citizen, Hokubei Mainichi, New Directions, The Clipper, The Writer's Forum, Topaz Times, Trek, All Aboard,* and *Matrix.* Some of the stories were later compiled and published in *Yokohama, California* (The Caxton Printers, Ltd., 1949, and University of Washington Press, 1985) and in *The Chauvinist and Other Stories* (Asian American Studes Center, University of California, Los Angeles, 1979). The original publication date appears at the end of each selection. Russell Leong's interview with Toshio Mori was first published in *Amerasia Journal* (Vol. 7, No. 1, 1980). The Bancroft Library at the University of California, Berkeley, houses the Mori and Saroyan correspondences.

Our special thanks go to Steven Mori and Hisayo Mori for their support and generosity in providing access to previously unpublished material and photographs for this collection.

—PATRICIA WAKIDA

Foreword

Being a writer is one of the hardest professions one can choose for a living, my father used to tell me. He knew from experience, since he struggled all of his life to make ends meet, supporting his writing and his family by running a nursery and later working as a salesman for a wholesale florist. Despite its challenges, he loved writing, spending hours and days worrying about which words to use or not to use.

As a father, he was as idyllic as any all-American dad on television could be in the fifties. He played ball with me, took me to movies, encouraged my reading, watched TV with me, and was stern but understanding when I got into mischief, which was often. Since he worked at home during my childhood, he was always there when I needed him. I know that the literary world is probably missing some great stories because of my presence, but I don't think either of us would have traded those years for anything.

My father was known for his gentle, insightful stories about Japanese Americans, but he was far more complex than most people realize. He also wrote stories about other cultures, but they never sold. He tried his hand at writing greeting cards, but Hallmark turned him down. He wrote lyrics to a few songs as well, and since he could not afford to foot the bill for production costs, he lost one song to a record production scam. He was shut out of the deal and his song was plagiarized by other writers and became a moderate hit for a major recording star. He especially yearned to sell a story to *Playboy*, which showcased the best writers of the day, and he worked for years on erotic story ideas that were never finished to his own satisfaction.

One of my dad's most memorable anecdotes came in the early 1970s when old writing pal William Saroyan called up and asked to meet him for a brief visit because he was having a flat tire fixed in San Leandro. So my father, mother, and I jumped into our car and sped off to meet with the legendary scribe. In his inimitable eccentric fashion, Saroyan greeted us and began talking a mile a minute about his recent travels and travails, handing us an autographed book. Ten minutes later, he was back on the road, handlebar mustache curling up with a smile.

Just around that time, college students began to discover my father's stories. He started speaking at college campuses and struck up lasting friendships with the newer generation of Asian American writers. Despite failing health, he was finally gaining recognition for all of his hard work, after years of neglect. Thanks to all his friends and fans, his final years were among his best.

In 1980, I lost four of my heroes: John Lennon, Alfred Hitchcock, Steve McQueen... and my dad. Frail and weak after battling various illnesses for two years, my father suffered a fatal heart attack. He was at the height of his popularity. I still can't think of that year without crying.

In spite of all the hardships he endured (the relocation, the aftermath of war, supporting his aging parents, the shocking assassinations of the sixties, and the political scandal of the seventies), he was never bitter or cynical in his writing or in person. He was almost always upbeat, hoping that the tragedies would bring out the best in mankind and not the worst. Although my father was not overtly religious, he did believe in satori, the intuitive inner light that is most sought after in Zen Buddhism. Perhaps, the greatest compliment he ever gave me was telling me that I had already achieved it without even realizing it. Like my other heroes, past and present, my father certainly had satori in abundance.

—STEVEN Y. MORI

Introduction

Introduction
by Lawson Fusao Inada

I.

"Toshio Mori." Two words. Five syllables. "Toshio Mori." A nice ring to it. Easy to say. Remember. "Toshio Mori." A name. A person. "Toshio Mori." Son, brother, husband, father. "Toshio Mori." Author, colleague, friend.

"Toshio Mori, this is your desk."
"T-O-S-H-I-O M-O-R-I. Here is your card."
"We can count on this Toshio Mori."
"At shortstop, Toshio Mori."
"Toshio Mori gets here early."
"I bought this batch from Toshio Mori."
"Father, I'd like you to meet Toshio Mori."
"Let's publish this Toshio Mori."
"Did you read that Toshio Mori?"
"Who is this Toshio Mori?"
"We've got something in Toshio Mori."
"Hello, Toshio Mori?"
"Toshio Mori, you and your family…"
"Toshio Mori—how do you spell that?"
"I leased this from Toshio Mori."
"Toshio Mori, you've been assigned to…"
"Toshio Mori, we regret to inform you…"
"Toshio Mori! Long time no see!"
"I bought this batch from Toshio Mori."
"Toshio Mori gets here early."

"At long last, Toshio Mori…"
"You can count on Toshio Mori."
"Dear Toshio Mori: Unfortunately…"
"Toshio Mori?"
"Toshio Mori."
"It is our honor to present Toshio Mori."

II.

Toshio Mori, with the publication of his book of stories, *Yokohama, California*, was hailed in the introduction by famed author William Saroyan as the "first real Japanese American writer. He writes about the Japanese of California."[1] With such a writer and subject matter, this was no ordinary book but a historic literary event.

The year was 1949. The book was to have appeared in 1942, but its publication, as Saroyan said, was "postponed." But now it was available to the American public, and Toshio Mori was being graciously introduced—by a Pulitzer-prize-winning author, no less—onto the American literary scene.

1949. The United Nations building would be dedicated in New York; the Yankees would win the World Series; *South Pacific* would be a hit on Broadway; President Truman would introduce his domestic legislation, the "Fair Deal"; James Gould Cozzens would receive the Pulitzer price in fiction: America was booming, on the move. As Toshio Mori stated in *Yokohama, California*: "The day is here and is Lil' Yokohama's day."

III.

But was "the day" really here? Had Mori's time arrived? Or was his book—written mostly in the late 1930s and early 1940s—"behind" the time? Or was it "ahead" of its time?

Mori, the professional nurseryman, the man of seasons—timely planting, timely harvesting—had to wonder about his literary timing. As did his publisher—for The Caxton Printers was not a big-time New York publishing firm that could afford to take chances. Rather, the company in Caxton, Idaho, was a small business off the literary map, with a little-known author who had written about a place not to be found on any map.

Moreover, during the "postponement," the war with Japan had happened. *Yokohama, California* by Toshio Mori. ("He writes about the Japanese of California.") How would the public respond?

To Caxton's credit, the book was published. That speaks of professional integrity, conviction in the merit of the author, and trust in the buying public. At the very least, Caxton could expect Mori's own people to embrace and support this endeavor—taking pride in this auspicious accomplishment by one of their own—and since California had become the most populous state in the nation, the regional readership was surely in place to welcome this fellow Californian, and from there the nation could receive this unique contribution to American letters by a vital, new American author. And, after all, it was 1949...

Despite mostly favorable reviews, sales were low, and the book slid into oblivion. And Toshio Mori, with gratitude for becoming an author, went about his business earning a living and supporting his family as a nurseryman. He continued to write, continued to submit materials for publication, but it was not until *three decades* later, with the rise of "ethnic awareness" and the founding of Asian American programs on campuses, that Toshio Mori was to be "discovered" and recognized by a limited public. His novel *Woman From Hiroshima* appeared in a limited edition in 1978, and a second collection of his stories, *The Chauvinist*, was published in 1979. Toshio Mori died in 1980.

IV.

The story of Toshio Mori—the person and literary personage—is inextricable from his people—a people who had been heaped with scorn and regarded with contempt since their arrival on the shores of America. They were not so much "people" as a labor force—hands and bodies suitable for field work and servitude. Yet, with their work ethic, acumen, and adaptability, they were difficult to control, much less be rid of.

They were clever and persistent as pests. They finagled ways to circumvent restrictions designed specifically for their kind; they took stands and fought back, yammering in broken English; they organized, hired lawyers for negotiation; they founded businesses and established a network of thriving communities. In actuality, they became exemplary of the American way; but they were—as was Japan, as was the Orient—

3

subject to not only disdain but hatred and fear, via the perceived threat of the "Yellow Peril" syndrome. Moreover, these "inscrutable" people had, with their "breeding habits," given birth to, if not "Americans," erstwhile American citizens.

This, then, is the milieu into which Toshio Mori was born in 1910, to immigrants—from Japan. At birth, considerable options were already beyond consideration. However, it can be said that the very circumstances and conditions of his birth and upbringing were to provide him with the sensitivity and sensibility that were to become his hallmark as a writer.

He had that "certain something"—the vision, intellect, heart, conviction, diligence—it took to make himself into a writer, and, against all odds. (Whoever heard of a Japanese American writer? Those people were the stuff of fiction—and outlandish fiction at that—not the *creators* of fiction.) After years of perseverance, he managed to break through the "color barrier" and become a bona fide, published, American author, culminating in the contract for publication of an entire volume of fiction.

Had World War II not happened, and if *Yokohama, California* had been published in 1942, as scheduled, the reception (or non-reception) may very well have been similar to what awaited it in 1949. That is, war or no war, Toshio Mori—and his people—were nevertheless what they were in the public eye, and no mere book would change that perception. Moreover, the war with Japan and the American internment of people of Japanese ancestry had, by 1949, added further dimensions to how Japanese Americans were perceived; there was a spotlight of scrutiny on the people; thus, it is understandable that Mori's own people would not necessarily welcome a book called *Yokohama, California* by a JAPanese American writer.

On a related note, one wonders how Mori's "ethnic" contemporaries were received and perceived by their respective communities for *their* "pioneering" efforts. For example, Richard Wright, the African American author, had his first collection of stories, *Uncle Tom's Children*, published in 1938. Or, Jose Antonio Villarreal had his work, *Pocho* (the first Mexican American novel), published in 1959. And both authors had "legitimate" status conferred upon them by big New York firms: Harper and Row, and Doubleday and Company.

Furthermore, one wonders how, in 1949, as companions to *Yokohama, California*, an "ethnic California" series would have fared, with titles such as *Canton, California, Chihuahua, California, Manila, California, Nairobi, California, Nuremberg, California, Oglala, California, Palermo, California, Warsaw, California*, and so on. Or, how would such a series be greeted today?

Today, the best-known "Japanese American" work is *Snow Falling On Cedars* by David Guterson; the best-known "American Indian" author is Tony Hillerman. John Howard Griffin's *Black Like Me* (Griffin disguised himself as black and documented the experience) became a big seller and award-winner in the 1960s. One wonders, then, if a book titled *Inside Yokohama, California* by a "Ted Martin" just might have been a big seller in 1949.

V.

Toshio Mori—
the "first real Japanese
American writer"

"First" is a historical designation; Mori was a founder; others come after the *first*. "Real" is a designation for the authentic, the genuine; Mori was certainly *real*. "Japanese" can be a superficial label, or it can be deeply ingrained—the language, customs, social ethics, spiritual values, and cultural aesthetics of Mori's upbringing were *Japanese*. "American" also aptly applies to Mori—his public school education, his love of baseball, his rise from humble origins to become a self-made, successful businessman and a self-taught, published author all exemplify what it means to be an *American*. "Writer" designates a literary personage and a proven entity; there are those who write, and then there are those like Toshio Mori: *writer*.

In retrospect, it might be seen that Toshio Mori is not to be so conveniently and conventionally categorized by that five-word phrase. It might eventually be realized that there was genius and greatness to this unassuming nurseryman, this farmer of flowers who managed to write at night. The reputation of Toshio Mori may well blossom posthumously, in the manner of Vincent van Gogh (with his sunflowers) and Emily

Dickinson (with her garden). And, as the major African American musical innovators of the twentieth century may one day receive rightful recognition, so may Toshio Mori.[2]

The "first" may come to be regarded as a "foremost," and an artist of *international* stature and relevance. And in this era of impersonal technology and pervasive escapism, Mori's stories of "village life" may find resonance in the "global village," for even in high-rise conditions, life persists on the local scale of interpersonal relationships, with local commerce and the spirit of neighborliness. And real stories, as with real flowers, have yet to be rendered obsolete.

And the stories of Toshio Mori, taken as a whole, provide a colorful and panoramic "mural" of his beloved locale. The people loom large as life, engaged in the archetypal experiences and passages of life; they are Japanese Americans, certainly and specifically, but also individual humans with all the hopes and fears, conflicts and struggles common to humanity: they embody what it means to be alive.

Thus, the "mural" radiates with an inner glow—the enduring, timeless, and timely soul and spirit of the people. Mori's gift was to value his people—to appreciate and respect the "common," and to recognize the eventful in the day-to-day. And as Mori was very much a creation of his community, he reciprocated by creating art of his community:
> *Yokohama, California* by Toshio Mori;
> Toshio Mori by Yokohama, California.

VI.

The Brothers Murata, published here for the first time, comes as a stunning surprise. It is a novel-length work, apparently completed in 1944,[3] and it is as if the residents of Yokohama, California, have been transplanted in the desert of "Yokohama, Utah"—the Central Utah Relocation Camp called Topaz. This novel set in Topaz may very well be the only such work to be written in an American concentration camp.[4]

The fact that it was written at all speaks to the conscience, responsibility, and dedication of Toshio Mori. And far from being a departure from the Mori milieu, the novel is actually in keeping with his integral approach as a writer—that of being an "observer," as he put it—and, fittingly enough, Mori writes of his community and its people.

But conditions have changed. It is as if the glowing "mural" of Yokohama, California, has been radically vandalized and defaced, almost beyond recognition. The colors have been replaced, reduced to a black-white-gray starkness in the manner of Picasso's "Guernica," and the representational realism has been distorted to an angular expressionism verging on surrealism: porches and storefronts have been transformed to bleak, black barracks jutting helter-skelter on barren ground; at first glance, this setting may appear to be a low-lying housing project, but in the far reaches of the background hovers what resembles the White House or Capitol Hill obscured by clouds of dust, and in the foreground is a barbed-wire fence upon which, upon closer inspection, are shreds of paper, pierced by barbs, containing fragments of print: "We hold these truths...," "We the people...," "Instructions to all persons of Japanese ancestry...." And most striking of all, there are no people depicted in this "mural," but thousands upon thousands of five-digit numbers, like "19228," scattered about in swarms, like insects.

This is the setting, then, for *The Brothers Murata*. And, as the story commences, real people do emerge, in true Mori fashion, to go about their lives—there is domesticity, and there are the day-to-day struggles and relationships; however, there is also a specific, volatile issue for all to confront.

The Brothers Murata, although a work of fiction, is both historic *and* prophetic, for the issue it concerns resounds in "camp" communities to this day.[5] And perhaps for that reason—"controversy"—it went unpublished; now, however, long after the dark "episode" of internment, scarcely acknowledged in America, the novel arises to cast a haunting light on conflict anywhere.

VII.

Steven Mori, Toshio's son, says of this father: "He loved writing." And that phrase is the key to all of Toshio Mori's writing: He loved writing. And that love of writing transfers in the writing to love of life. Time and again that love is felt in the stories—that feeling of appreciation, warmth, and wonder emanating from the printed page.

In the story "The Sweet Potato," it is the day that is cherished, moment to moment, for this is the last day of the Golden Gate

International Exposition, the world's fair staged on Treasure Island in San Francisco Bay. Seventeen million visitors had attended the fair since its opening in 1939; the closing date was September 2, 1940, for this "Pageant of the Pacific."[6]

The story, in Mori's manner, is not so much one of action but reflection: two young men stroll about the grounds, bantering, and then have tea. The fair itself may be said to be the "main character," for it was staged to commemorate the completion of both the San Francisco–Oakland Bay Bridge and the Golden Gate Bridge, and to celebrate San Francisco's prominence in trade with Asia. An international atmosphere pervades, exemplified by the men sharing a table at the Japanese Tearoom with a white woman and her son. It turns out the woman speaks Japanese, from having taught in Yokohama. The very venue is conducive to conversation, and the fair itself has brought these people together—mother and son with those "long secluded in the Japanese community."

There is regret for the end of the fair, for it represents how life could be in the world, with peace and mutuality. All in all, a graceful and subdued story, perhaps the only one to take place in this momentous setting—and it took a Japanese American writer to perceive and grasp the significance at all.

For that's not all; beneath the deceptively placid surface, and beyond the horizon, the real "action" is taking place—war is raging in Europe, and Japan is waging war in Asia. Thus, this "last day" is certainly to be cherished, "forgetting time and place," for the time is September, 1940; Treasure Island is about to become a major naval base; and there is more than fall in the air.

In "1936," another inimitable Mori reflection, philosophical and poetic, he says "I am in love with it"—the year, and life—and "as uncertain as our lives may be we have come more to love the days that are ours." Even a Monday, a workday, is a "day of adventures," and he describes a very brief incident "that makes Mondays memorable." In a very real sense, the title can be updated to the current year, for what Mori expresses is applicable to now.

He loved writing. With his hard-won mastery of English, his self-taught, masterful technique and style, his ability to write must have been a continual source of wonder and amazement to him. And with his love of writing, there must have been a concurrent love of reading, studying international classics—of literature and philosophy in the curriculum of "Mori University."

He loved writing. With his inherent talent, he must have felt chosen to write—it was a gift not to squander, but to treasure, nurture; thus, his determination to write assiduously at night. He loved writing. By day, he must have thought, "Tonight I *get* to write." And after a full day of tending to plants—nurturing sprouts, weeding, trimming, thinning to increase quality—it surely brought a smile to his face as he "sprouted" rows of words that would need editing. He loved writing. It must have felt like a privilege, a welcome challenge, to be able to reflect in depth, to be able to express impressions, valued insights, to be able to formulate, synthesize on paper, to be able to create lyrical, moving, truthful passages from scratch; it must have been an act of affirmation; and, with his depth of spirituality, it must have been a form of meditation. He loved writing. And the prospect of sharing his "harvest" was surely of great joy to him.

He loved writing. And as the father gazes at his son, the photographer, in the cover photo, the "unfinished message" is in the very eyes of this man called Toshio Mori: He loved.

NOTES

1. Early on, William Saroyan, the first "real" Armenian American writer, recognized Mori's talent and championed his career. Saroyan's introduction appears in both editions of *Yokohama, California* (The Caxton Printers, 1949, and University of Washington Press, 1985).

2. Earl "Fatha" Hines, the first real modern-jazz pianist, resided in Oakland from the 1950s to his death in 1983.

3. The date is uncertain—1944 was suggested in the introduction to *The Chauvinist and Other Stories*, while Steven Mori refers to the manuscript simply as "very old."

4. For an in-depth look at the experiences of Japanese Americans during

World War II, see *Only What We Could Carry* (ed. Lawson Inada), Heyday Books (2000).

5. Mori's novel is directly related to the late John Okada's novel, *No-No Boy* (Tuttle, 1957), which received a reception similar to *Yokohama, California*'s. Okada was also "discovered" in the 1970s, and his novel was reprinted at the personal expense of the editors of the Asian American anthology *Aiiieeeee!* (Penguin Books USA, Inc.); *No-No Boy* is now available from the University of Washington Press. The fact that both major authors converged, during different decades, on a singular issue attests to the significance of that issue.

6. For a more detailed description, see *Endangered Dreams* (Oxford University Press), by Kevin Starr, State Librarian of California. The fair was the last and greatest of its kind, providing public access to the likes of Diego Rivera, Georgia O'Keeffe, and the Count Basie Orchestra with Lester Young. Among attendees, the Inada family from Fresno.

Through Anger and Love

Through Anger and Love

From a parked automobile Haruo stuck his head out a little and peered across the street. Yes, he was still standing by the entrance talking to several men. His old man was talking and laughing as if nothing had happened yesterday. Had he forgotten already? No, his old man couldn't forget that easily. Haruo cautiously drew back and sat on the fender. Five minutes to seven by the City Hall clock. Promptly at seven, he knew, the flower market was going to open. What should he buy? What flowers were most popular, and most profitable? Suddenly he heard footsteps approaching the car. Instantly he was on his feet, and without looking back scurried around the corner. Safely past the corner he increased his pace. At a hundred yards he began to puff with exertion and slackened a bit. Just ahead he spied an alley and ran for it. Puffing and coughing he rested his nine-year-old body, his eyes trained on the sidewalk. Two minutes passed and nobody came after him. Slowly he came out and looked down the street and sighed with relief.

The market was open by now. Well, let the others go in first. He would walk around the block and take his time. Unhurriedly he stopped and looked at the store windows. Every now and then he looked up and down the street. Watching his chance he would slip into the market and make his purchase. He must look out for his old man. Then he must act natural when buying from the wholesalers so they would think that he was buying for his old man. Several minutes ago he was unsure of himself. He couldn't believe that he would be able to go through with it. Now he was sure of himself. He knew what flowers to get and where to get them. His father bought a lot of things from Matsumoto and

Toscana. Matsumoto was a grower of carnations and Toscana raised roses. They knew him well. It would be easy. If only his old man would not appear at the wrong time.

Nearing the market once more Haruo slowed down. His eyes darted from the market entrance to the adjoining wholesale stores. Cautiously he stepped behind the row of parked cars watching for his father. He was not in sight. Should he take a chance now or wait awhile? He watched a number of people coming in and out of the market. Flower business must have been good yesterday. Almost all the florists were present. Should he hurry and buy before the flowers were all gone? Several more florists came out with armfuls of flowers. Haruo became desperate. He hurriedly crossed the street to a spot near the entrance. Growing bolder he peered through the window, watching all sides, and then he saw his father.

His father was in the rear of the market purchasing cyclamen and mixed plants. He looked very much absorbed in the plants. Should he slip in now? Haruo could see Matsumoto, whose table was near the entrance. At least he could get the carnations. Wait a minute. He became suspicious, cautious. Was his old man purposely in the rear so he would fall in a trap? Maybe his old man had seen him a few minutes ago and asked Matsumoto to look out for him. That would be terrible. Then he would have to go back home crawling on his knees. Undoubtedly his father would further humiliate him and kick him out of the house. Maybe Matsumoto did not know. He looked keenly at the carnation grower's face, watching for a telltale sign that he was looking out for his old man. No, he did not know. Matsumoto's face was calm and relaxed. His eyes did not shift about. Then he looked in the rear of the market, watching for his old man. He was not around. He was gone. Eagerly he walked in, heading straight for Matsumoto's table.

Haruo's face fell. Matsumoto's table was bare. Where did his flowers go? Did he sell out? He hesitated in his tracks. Matsumoto's eyes brightened.

"Hello, Haruo!" he cried. "How are you? My, you've grown. And how is your mother?"

"Fine," Haruo said hurriedly. He looked over the table. "Did you sell out? Have you any carnations left?"

"Do you want carnations?" Matsumoto asked. "Let's see. How many do you want?"

"Ten bunches," Haruo said eagerly.

The man looked under the table and started unwrapping a big bundle. "All right, Haruo," he said. "I'll give you ten. Mixed colors?"

"Yes, but give me lots of red."

Matsumoto laughed heartily and his belly shook. "You're a smart boy, Haruo. You know what sells."

Haruo looked about. Matsumoto laughed and talked too loud. He must get away. "Will you please wrap it up?"

"Are you going to take it with you now or is your father coming to pick it up?" he asked.

"I want it now," Haruo said quickly.

Matsumoto hummed a tune and took his time wrapping. Finally he handed over the package. "All right, Haruo."

"How much is it?" Haruo asked.

"Dollar and a half. I'm charging you only fifteen cents a bunch."

"Pay you next time," Haruo said.

"Sure. That's all right," Matsumoto cried, waving his hand.

Haruo fairly ran to Toscana's table. He must hurry. His father might return any minute. His eyes brightened at the sight of Toscana's good roses piled high on his table.

"Hello, boy," called the Italian. "Do you want to buy nice roses? I'll give you a bargain today."

Haruo picked up a bunch to see if the outer petals of the roses were bruised, and then, satisfied, examined the bases of the stems for the telltale mark of old flowers. Toscana chuckled and picked up several bunches for Haruo to examine.

All fresh flowers, my boy. No kidding," he said. "You want to buy for your papa?"

"How much?" Haruo asked hurriedly.

Toscana counted off six bunches. "Two dollars to you. A real bargain."

"I'll take it," he said quickly.

Haruo looked about while he waited for the man to finish wrapping. He must get away. Any minute now his old man would be coming back.

Which entrance should he take, the front or the rear? Eagerly he accepted the package from Toscana.

"All right, boy," the nurseryman said, nodding and smiling.

With both arms loaded with packages Haruo walked off excitedly. He must hurry. He must catch a bus and ride back to his district and start selling his flowers. He quickened his little strides in the direction of the rear entrance. Suddenly from the front entrance came a familiar cry, "Haruo! Come back! Haruo!"

Terror-stricken, he broke for the rear door. Gripping his bundles tight to his sides he ran past several tables, not heeding the cries. Reaching the sidewalk he cut sharply to his right and then across the street. He must not be caught. It would be the end of him. He must get away. Running swiftly around the corner he headed for Seventh. He must shake his father off his trail. Should he go up or down Seventh? He must go up to reach the bus line, but suppose his old man was waiting for him at the next block? No, that wouldn't do. Should he run straight for First and wait around the pier, and later retrace his steps? That would be loss of time. No, he must go down Seventh and walk back to Twelfth. Then he remembered the jitney running on Seventh and his eyes brightened. His father would never think of the jitney.

To make sure his old man was not following, Haruo ran a couple of blocks more and headed for Sixth. At the corner of Sixth he sat puffing on the gutter looking in all directions, expecting the appearance of his father. Anxiously he looked to see if the flowers were bruised and the stems broken. They looked all right, and his anxiety turned to relief. He must sell them before noon while they were in good condition. In the afternoon they would start wilting without water.

Five minutes went by and his father did not appear. Cautiously he walked back to Seventh and waited for the jitney. Time after time he hid among the buildings whenever a figure appeared on the street. When the jitney came he boarded quickly and asked for a transfer. He slid low in his seat so he would not be noticed from the street. Several times the driver stopped the car for passengers. Haruo held his breath at every stop, expecting his father to jump aboard. At Clay the jitney turned left and passed Eighth, Ninth, and Tenth. He noticed the tall buildings coming into view. Three more blocks and he must get off and catch his bus.

Maybe he should get off a block away and make sure his old man wasn't waiting at the spot. Scrambling to his feet he asked the driver to stop at the next corner.

No sight of his old man. He walked eagerly to the corner of Thirteenth and Clay for his bus. He wished the bus would hurry. Several minutes of waiting brought restlessness and uneasiness. Was the bus never coming? Then he caught sight of it in the distance. At last!

Safely on the bus and bound for his district, Haruo leaned back with relief. His father would never find him now. With his feet on the front seat Haruo braced himself. His shoes did not reach the floor. Every now and then he looked into the packages to see if the flowers were all right. A dollar and a half to Matsumoto and two dollars to Toscana. He must pay them next time. He must sell pretty nearly all his flowers to make a good profit. He had ten bunches of carnations and six bunches of roses. That would mean twenty dozen carnations and twelve dozen roses. He must sell cheaper than his old man. How much should he charge? Twenty-five cents a dozen for carnations and thirty-five cents a dozen for roses would be a bargain. Anybody would buy at that price. First, he would go to the shops in the district that knew him. Mazzini, the Browns, Nick, Hamilton Hardware, Rosloff Service Station, Riley, Joe, and the rest. They were friends of his old man. They would be glad to see him.

Haruo took out his pencil and pad and figured. The car moved and vibrated. Several times the flowers started to slip off the seat. Twenty dozens at twenty-five cents a dozen would be five dollars. Twelve dozen roses at thirty-five would amount to four dollars. Nine dollars for the day! That would be swell. He would give his uncle fifty cents a day for room and board.

The bus stopped and lurched. Haruo looked out of the window. Pretty soon he must get off. He put his pencil and pad in his pocket. He had better start selling right away. He must make good today. If he failed and had to go back begging for forgiveness his old man would laugh at him and give him a stick. No, he couldn't fail. When a boy has run away from home for good he should not think of going home. Even if it killed him he shouldn't. He should move on and take the consequences.

Gripping the packages tightly, he waited for his block. Familiar buildings came into view. The Woolworth, Safeway, Gibson Drug, Palace

Theater, Texaco Station, and Bank of America. His eyes brightened and he eagerly went forward to be let off. He could see Rosloff gingerly wiping a customer's windshield. He could see that the Browns were doing a good business. He smiled. His hometown.

Haruo got off at the next corner. For a moment he stood bewildered and hesitating. What was his plan? Where should he go first? Again the dread of uncertainty and the fear of his future shook his nerve. Did he do right by leaving home? Was he at fault and not father? How did the quarrel begin? His cheeks burned at the thought of it. Last night his father slapped him in the face in front of his brothers and sisters and called him a fool. His brothers laughed and his sisters looked with astonishment. They saw him crying, and the hard shaking he got in addition. What did he do? He had done nothing. What was it? He didn't know. The quarrel began a long time ago. He must be bad, or his old man mistaken? Was it his quick temper or his father's? He leaned against the telephone pole wondering what to do. Suppose the folks did not want to buy flowers today? Suppose he couldn't sell enough to pay back Matsumoto and Toscana? He would be in a fix. He couldn't live at his uncle's any length of time without paying room and board. Then he heard Rosloff's familiar voice calling, "Hello there, sonny! Come over here!"

Haruo eagerly ran across the street, his packages dangling. "How are you, Haruo?" asked the service station man. "What you got there?"

"Flowers," Haruo said eagerly. "Carnations and roses. Would you like to buy some, Mr. Rosloff?"

He laid the packages on the ground and quickly unwrapped one of them. He held a bunch of carnations in each hand. "They're nice and fresh, and a bargain. Twenty-five cents a dozen."

The man laughed. "Come inside of the station," he said. "You don't want the sun on your flowers."

Inside his cool office Rosloff picked up red and white carnation bunches. "These are swell flowers."

Haruo nodded his head. He was busy unwrapping the other bundle. "I have some nice roses too. They're thirty-five a dozen."

"Are these your dad's or your own?" the man asked.

"They're my flowers. I'm selling them," Haruo replied.

"Your dad was here five minutes ago," Rosloff said.

Haruo looked quickly at his friend. He could not tell what the man meant by it. He kept still, busying himself with the flowers.

"I'll take a dozen of pink roses and a dozen each of red and white carnations," the man said. "I'm going to take them home and surprise my wife."

"Gee, thanks!" Haruo's eyes danced as he cut the strings of the bunches and started counting.

The man took a seat and examined a headlight globe. "You cut school today, Haruo?" he asked casually.

Haruo did not look up. He kept counting the flowers slowly. "Yes, I was busy this morning."

"You should be busy in school," Rosloff quietly said. "Let your father sell flowers and worry about money."

"I can't."

"Why?" The man carefully laid the globe on the shelf.

Haruo handed over the carnations and the roses to Rosloff. Hurriedly he wrapped his remaining flowers. "I can't tell you, Mr. Rosloff."

"Did you have a fight with your dad?"

Haruo nodded his head.

"Pshaw! That's all right, son. Forget it," Rosloff said. "Sometimes you've got to taste vinegar, and sometimes honey. That's the way it goes, Haruo, whether you're young or old."

He stood shifting his weight from one foot to the other.

"Oh, I forgot, Haruo. How much do you want?"

"Eighty-five cents," Haruo said.

The man opened the register and counted the money.

"Mr. Rosloff, please don't tell my father I was here," Haruo begged. "I've run away from home."

"I won't squeal on you," the man said. "You can depend on me."

Outside Haruo stepped along gingerly, his coins jingling in the pants pocket. Eighty-five cents to the good. A swell start. With luck he might make nine dollars. He hummed a tune. He'll show his father. This was his world. Why had he been afraid several minutes ago? He knew flowers. He liked flowers. Where did his fear come from? He laughed and wondered where to try next. Up ahead, the Browns' two shops bustled with activity. Miss Brown's stationery shop always had customers. She was nice to everybody. He would go in there next. Maybe her father, who ran a cigar-stand next door, would also buy flowers.

Haruo walked in and found a lot of customers at the counters. Almost instantly he was the center of attention. He smiled gratefully to Miss Brown, who ordered him to open the packages. People cluttered about him. A lady wanted a dozen mixed carnations. One old gentleman bought two dozen roses. A young girl took a dozen carnations for her mother. Miss Brown purchased two dozen roses, and finally escorted him to her father's place. "Dad, why don't you buy some beautiful roses for mother?" she said. "He has some of the nicest colors."

Her father looked up from his work and examined the roses. He bought two dozens. Haruo walked away, his head high in the air. He chuckled and hummed. Flushed with confidence, he went in Mazzini's, Hamilton Hardware, Riley's, and Joe's Garage one right after another. When he came out of Joe's his packages were light. Four bunches of carnations and three bunches of roses left. His two pockets were bulging with small coins. How much had he made? He laughed. He must count the money. This was fun. Tomorrow he would take another portion of the town and keep rotating his route. He could go on forever. He smiled happily.

Haruo ran across the street to the park and sat under the shade of a tree. First, he tackled one pocketful of money and then the other. Three dollars and forty cents plus three dollars and sixty cents equals seven dollars. Seven dollars! He must have sold many dozens. Yes, sixteen dozen carnations and nine dozen roses. He could easily make nine dollars. He looked across the street at the bank clock. It was almost noon. His stomach felt empty. Nick's Cafe stood invitingly at the corner. Should he go in now and eat? He looked at the remaining carnations and roses. They were in pretty good condition. Yes, he could go in Nick's and eat and sell his flowers at the same time. He dumped his money in his pockets and picked up the flowers.

His hands bumped against the bulging pockets as he walked, and his thoughts returned to his triumph. Nine dollars gross profit minus three dollars and fifty cents cost equals five dollars and fifty cents net profit. He could do it. It meant freedom and pride. He could do as he pleased.

On the way to Nick's he stopped short in front of a maroon Ford DeLuxe. It looked familiar. There was no one in it and he looked closely at the license plate. Quickly his eyes darted about the stores expecting to see his old man. His easy, springy stride of a moment ago became short hesitant steps. Somewhere in town his father was making his rounds. Where could he be? Suppose his father caught him by surprise? A look of terror crossed his face. He must get rid of his flowers right away and slip away from the district. Every few yards Haruo looked across the street and behind him, expecting his father to jump out of hiding. Hurriedly he looked in Nick's. His father wasn't there. He felt hungry, he swallowed his saliva. He could go for three hamburger sandwiches, a pie, and a glass of milk. Cautiously Haruo stood at the corner and peered inside Nick's to make sure his father wasn't among the customers. Satisfied he crossed the street for Nick's.

At the doorway Haruo hesitated. Was he taking a chance? Suppose his father should come in while he was eating and grab a hold of him? His father would surely explode and soundly spank him in front of Nick and everybody. No, he mustn't take such a risk. First, he would go around the block and see if his father was in any of the stores. Then he would hurry back, order just a hamburger, and move on.

All around the block Haruo looked in every shop. He was sure that his father wasn't nearby. He broke into a run. Perhaps he could eat a piece of pie if he hurried. That would be swell. A banana cream or pineapple. He mustn't forget to ask Nick about the flowers. Maybe some of his customers would also make purchases.

Breathlessly he ran in the cafe and carefully laid his packages in the corner. First he saw Nick, who broadly grinned at him. "Hello, young man!" he cried. "How are you?" Then he noticed his father sitting and facing him, with his small gimlet eyes studying him and a sly smile. For a second Haruo stood open-mouthed, and then backed away quickly to the corner to pick up the packages and run outside.

"Haruo!" cried his father, smiling and holding up his hand. "Haruo, come back here."

Haruo hesitated. His father was still sitting leisurely. He could get away easily. He could run out, hide, and never allow his father to touch him. There was danger in remaining. Still he hesitated.

"Come here, Haruo. How are you doing?" his father said. "Business good today?"

Haruo slowly approached his father. "I made seven dollars already," he said.

"Good! You're doing fine," his father said. "Sit down here, Haruo, and let's have lunch together."

"What'll you have, young man?" Nick asked.

Haruo sat down, looking cautiously at his father. "I want a hamburger and a banana cream pie," he said.

Nick went away to fill the order. His father looked in the corner. "You still have some flowers to sell?" he asked.

Haruo nodded. "I have four bunches of carnations and three bunches of roses left."

"You sell them easily," his father said cheerfully. "Over seven dollars for the day. Not bad. I know you could earn it every day. You're pretty smart."

Nick came back with the order.

"Let's eat, Haruo," his father said. "I like Nick's hamburgers best. They're always good. How about you, Haruo?"

Haruo nodded his head while his mouth bit into the sandwich.

"I don't worry about you, Haruo," said his father. "No, sir. You can go out in the world today, and I know you can make a living. But your mama. She's worried about you. She wants you to come home. You don't want to worry her, Haruo."

Haruo sat silently munching his hamburger. He glanced at his father, who smiled back. Nick whistled and watched the hamburgers sizzle in the pans. A noon whistle went off at the factory several blocks away. Presently people cluttered in Nick's. All around him Haruo listened to the talk of business and of labor. He listened importantly to their talk and watched his banana cream disappear.

"Anything else, young man?" Nick asked him.

Haruo smiled and shook his head. His father got up and paid the bill.

"Come home when you're through selling the flowers. Mama will be expecting you," his father said. "I have to go home now and watch the store. You take your time, Haruo."

His father went away. Haruo sat sipping his milk and listened to the men talking of inflation, civil liberties, and sports. When he was finally through with his lunch Nick came over and bought a dozen carnations. "Goodbye, young man," were the departing words of Nick.

Outside Haruo walked up and down the main street carrying his packages without attempting to sell a bunch. The sun shone brightly. This was a swell day. A swell day to go to the ball park and see the Oaks and the Seals tangle. No, it was a greater day than that. He could leap, sing, and run all the way home. This was something he had never before experienced. This was a great thrill. Then he remembered his greatest disappointment, bitterness, and loneliness of last night as a prelude to joy. His warm laughing face became solemn. Suddenly tears filled his eyes. He wiped his tears with his sleeves and wondered if the people were noticing him in such a condition.

—1950

1936

1936

There is something in the way I feel toward the year 1936 that I shall be sure to remember. Perhaps it may be that I am living today, that I am alive and am striving toward my hope, that I feel so strongly the tang and the bracing weather of today and the more todays to come. It is the year I shall recall later as the time of change in the conduct of life and outlook. I'd like to explain away the change and the song of it here but that is a hopeless task just now. I must simply say it is the year of 1936 and was the year and let it go at that. But if I should tell you how I feel today about 1936, I might be able to do something about it.

I began suddenly or slowly, it does not matter, to want, to desire, to sink my teeth into everything I could grasp, to everything I see, hear, smell, taste, etc. I wanted to do everything, I wanted to know women, I wanted to know the white people, the minds of my generation and people, the Nisei, the nature of our parents, the Issei, the culture of Japan, the culture of America, of life as a whole. I wanted to go from the country to the city and from the city to the country. I began to move, I began by joining the Eden Japanese American Citizens League, I went to the girls' homes, I went to see the boys, listened to the lecture of Dr. Alfred Adler, the psychoanalyst, listened to Kagawa in English at the Oakland Auditorium, and also in Japanese at Wanto Gakuen. I listened to the Japanese girl talking about her beautiful girlfriend, Tsuyuko, who is wealthy and unhappy; the Tsuyuko I could not forget. I heard her speak of another girl who had been raised and educated in Japan, called over by the parents to join them in California. I heard of the girl who had ruined her chance for marriage and livelihood in America by her

27

temperament and objections, and was now returning to Japan on the next boat. I heard my friend speak of her friend as strong-willed who finally broke down and wept before the sailing day. She was afraid of her friend's rash nature and of her decision to return to Japan and the consequent fate. As I listened to the girl, of her life, gossip, experiences, talks, rumors, I saw how much I did not know of life, the limitations of my life, and how much more she was close to the life of the people and of herself. This girl (I have been grateful to her ever since) drove me restless with her knowledge and her life, to seek, to experience something of my own.

I do not know when I began or, perhaps, I do not know when I began to notice, to really notice the lives and the people inhabiting today in the year of 1936. I do not know exactly who or what event was the first experience; the lives and the people of 1936 are so assembled together, alike in usefulness, that I cannot place one individual or the individuals above another but must recall them together, hand in hand.

From the morning I began visiting the Japanese dentist in the heart of the downtown district, to have my teeth fixed, the every day, the days that come around simply and plainly every day, became my interest and love. I thought it lovely that each day became an adventure; I thought it lovely enough when I realized that every day, plain and simple, was unlike any other day. One day I would meet the white elevator girl who would take me up to the dentist's floor and she would say something about the weather, or about the dentist visiting, or about the tasty smell coming into the elevator shaft from the candy kitchen in the basement, and then I would not meet her for days.

On another day I might be riding home on the bus and would sit alongside a middle-aged man and a college student as I have precisely done. I would find out, as I watched the middle-aged man striking up a conversation with the college student, that he was a writer, a writer of cowboy stories, who had sold a half-dozen stories or so to the magazines. And I would listen to his theories and his battles with writing in the evenings, and listening, I would begin to think about his office (presumably an office man) and his family. I did not meet the same college student again but listening to that one conversation just before noonday, I found out he was once interested in writing but now had quit. He was a quiet youth, gentlemanly and of generous nature. The day and the meeting, and the impression would end just that way and I knew it was the end of another day. And with the weather of the days I found it the same. One day it would be warm, another day too hot for comfort, some days cloudy, another time windy, cold or raining, foggy, drizzling. To go further, it is true that a single day is a variation of temperature, light, etc., and I thought this was a lovely way of prolonging interest in life, to desire something that is yet to be and is not so sure about becoming that way, that uncertain as our lives may be we have come more to love the days that are ours.

While I was crazily pursuing everything, everything in life, wanting to know, wanting to experience, wanting to see the spark and the lives of men, wanting to see the spark of life and the spark of individuals, I could have been a poet. I could have claimed the stars and the universe, the earth, the soil, the birds, and the gentlefolks. Today I am not the same; I am still pursuing, still crazily lusting, but I do not and cannot claim the stars and the universe, the earth and the like, or even more so claim the women, the nations, the wealth, the patents, and the life. I cannot claim, when I come to think of it, even the petty things and I cannot claim the tools, I cannot claim the materials and the art of life. This is so I cannot claim the year of 1936 though I am in love with it, though I am glad I am living today. I simply sit here in my den, in the presence of the year 1936, present with its shortness, death, and variation, and also, conscious of the rarity, 1936, the only year to be 1936. This leads me to the ending, to the finish of this piece and the commencement of the brother years 1937, 1938, 1939, 1940, and so on, wanting to know everything, restless, hungering, seeking, crazily....

It is just as well to end anything like this on Monday of his life as well as on Saturday. It is the same, the ending and the beginning, and I shall take one day, Monday, the representative of all the Mondays, and the representative of Tuesdays, Wednesdays, Thursdays, Fridays, Saturdays, Sundays, and of the year 1936, as the spokesman, the chronicle, the record, and as, perhaps, a farce.

I will begin easily for myself, thinking from the time I rise for the flower market to work, thinking as I go along, remembering, tasting, visioning the faces I've seen and the events that were to be Monday. I will go to the market to sell flowers from 7 A.M. to 8:30 A.M. and finishing that I am through at the market, free to go home and turn over the soil, water the plants, cut the flowers, etc. On Mondays I cannot go home early; it is the day of adventures, because I am going to the dentist, and because there are many hours to fill between the market work and the dentist's appointment. The first thing I do when I am free for the morning (I notice) is go to the public library on Fourteenth and Grove. It is fascinating to see people reading, and it is fascinating to realize that here one can become learned and be up-to-date as anywhere else. But meeting the man, the incident that happened today on Monday that makes Mondays memorable, did not happen upstairs or downstairs in the reading room nor in the fiction room, the non-fiction room, but down the hall on the first floor in the men's rest room. I do not remember precisely the beginning of my chat with this man, the custodian of the library halls. He was leaning against the wall puffing his cigarette rapidly, taking time out for a smoke when I entered the place and our conversation began. He was my size, a small man, quite bald, a man you would not believe had gone a foot out of California or Oakland even. He began talking, and the minute he opened his mouth I knew he was anxious to have someone to talk to. He began talking of his days at sea and I was surprised at the news, surprised that the custodian of a public library could ever think of such an adventure of life.

"I have been on the sea for twenty years," he said. "I have been to many ports of the world, Bombay, Liverpool, Marseilles, Yokohama, everywhere, coming in, going out, around the world. For twenty years I saw very little but the sea."

"Twenty years is a long time," I said. "You must love the sea very much."

"I did not love the sea," he said. "I was much more afraid to starve on land. I was afraid I could get no job of any kind, I was afraid of knowing nothing, and I was afraid of starving."

I shall not make up anything of the meeting; I will leave it alone. It happened as I told you and it ended briefly without the usual rounds of drinks. In fact there is nothing unusual to this meeting and there is nothing unusual about his twenty years on the sea; only the fact that we talked and were simply alive and warm, to talk, and to listen, wanting to know, wanting to give, that the incident became memorable, that I should be able to remember it today.

I was ten minutes late for the appointment and the Japanese dentist was waiting for me. I have been going to this dentist for almost a year and every time I step from the waiting room to the laboratory, I am reminded not of teeth-fixing, but something of the experience and the sensitiveness of this artist of molars. He is what Sherwood Anderson would call an old craftsman. I have listened to the philosophies of the philosophy, from the books to the philosophers, the scholars, priests, and the masters of the past and they are all right; I do not junk them. But coming here in the laboratory, in the presence of this small Japanese, I forget many things, I forget philosophies, the books. It is an experience like a moth flying toward the red-hot lamp; myself leaping kangaroo-like to shake hands and derive some good and warmth from this man, an alive one. With this in mind I forget my teeth and the dentist begins to possess my teeth, till the teeth, my teeth, belong back and forth, from one to the other, belonging to the wanting-to-know, belonging to the wanting-to-give, till the teeth of the world (becoming the materials) become one taken possession of, taken care of, becoming relative one and all.

This is not what we talk of, the dentist and I, but if we were able to grease our tongues smoother and nobler, I think, since we are men, and alive today, it would be how we feel about the teeth, about love, about work, about hope, about life.

Every time I visit my brother's shop in Oakland I remember the unidentified day when I had a haircut at Tony's in the presence of two customers. This was out in the suburbs. There are times when I see Tony out on the sidewalk walking back and forth, wearing the barber's apron, smoking a cigar. He would wave his hand when he saw me. Sometimes when I went slow he would shout, "Hello, boy! Where are you going?"

"Hello, Tony," I said, "Oakland."

He would wave his hand again and smile. The day I am particular about was such a day as this. I went in for a haircut. Before I was there five minutes, two customers came in a minute apart. I remember this meeting at the barber shop because Tony and his two latest customers and myself were present and responsible for the effect. It is why I also remember that the event has something in common with my brother in his new rooms above his shop. The four of us at the barber shop did not talk about anything important, I remember. The Spaniard was kidding Tony about the warmth of the shop. (This was in December and Tony had a tiny coal-oil stove burning for heat.) All the while the two, the Spaniard and the Italian, kidded back and forth. In the corner a big Mexican was smiling and I, Japanese, sat in the chair smiling. I could not make up the nationalities present there that afternoon at the barber shop. The moment I caught on to the bizarreness of the meeting, the novelty of four nationalities assembled in one tiny shop, I began to think of America. This was not a new thing to the old stock of America but to me as a Japanese American, it was something. If one tiny barber shop could have four nationalities at one time, how many does America house? Then, I could believe the vastness and the goodness of America's project; this is the place, the earth where the brothers and the races meet, mingle and share, and the most likely place, the most probable part of the earth to seek peace and goodwill through relations with the rest of the world. It is for this reaction I think of my brother, living in his new surroundings, in the city, among the peoples of the earth, rooming in the same house with half-a-dozen nationalities, among them a Russian doctor, his best friend. I think of his life ahead in the city of America, I think of the thousands of untouched relations between the nationalities, the colors, the creeds, and the hour, the time and his opportunity of being.

I met Sheldon Brown's father in the morning of a Monday in 1936 and I shall end my day, my 1936, with the remembrance of Sheldon's dad because it is fitting, and for the reason that the meeting took place in the morning of my 1936 which is the afternoon, the evening of my piece and also the morning again. I had known Sheldon and his brother Bob since grammar-school days in Oakland. That was fifteen years ago; it does not concern here, today. I want to say something of Sheldon's father, who came to see me, a friendly visit, and we began talking about his sons, my friends. And the father of these two boys, now grown, twenty-seven and twenty-four respectively, laughed and chuckled as he related the uncertain and certain, an interesting career of the younger son. Bob, he related, believed he had found the medium, the business of his life, in acting, to be an actor. "After three years of college," the father chuckled and was amused at his son's notions, "he wants to be an actor. He is, today, studying dramatics, earning his bread as an art model in San Francisco."

"That is fine," I said to the father. He laughed heartily and one could see he had taken a fancy to Bob's ambition. The family, he said, would not interfere. It is no use; Bob tried his hand at carpentry (his father's trade), and was indifferent in interest and work. The father was skeptical of Bob's life, career, and the last I saw of him (the father), in 1936, with his amused, chuckling face, he was fancying and thrilling at the new generation with their struggles, soberliness, loneliness, that is, of 1936.

All this will be forgotten, about Sheldon's father and how Bob rose or fell, how at one time such and such a thing happened and that there ever was a year called 1936, and that there ever was a writer for its days, and that the people of 1936 were once living. All this will be forgotten; this is logical, this is not important. But what I am trying to get at, to put over to you, is that in 1936 once there was a youth wanting to know, wanting to know so badly he wanted to stab at everything, everything in life. He was living once, the youth of 1936, and is living again in 1937, 1938, and so on, till the time of man is no more. I am not weeping for him; I am glad for him, I cannot weep and feel sorry for something that is living and will be living long after our death.

—1936

Lil' Yokohama

Lil' Yokohama

In Lil' Yokohama, as the youngsters call our community, we have twenty-four hours every day… and morning, noon, and night roll on regularly just as in Boston, Cincinnati, Birmingham, Kansas City, Minneapolis, and Emeryville.

When the sun is out, the housewives sit on the porch or walk around the yard, puttering with this and that, and the old men who are in the house when it is cloudy or raining come out on the porch or sit in the shade and read the newspaper. The day is hot. All right, they like it. The day is cold. All right, all right. The people of Lil' Yokohama are here. *Here, here,* they cry with their presence, just like the youngsters when the teachers call the roll. And when the people among people are sometimes missing from Lil' Yokohama's roll, perhaps forever, it is another matter; but the news belongs here just as does the weather.

Today young and old are at the Alameda ball grounds to see the big game: Alameda Taiiku *vs.* San Jose Asahis. The great Northern California game is under way. Will Slugger Hironaka hit that southpaw from San Jose? Will the same southpaw make the Alameda sluggers stand on their heads? It's the great question.

The popcorn man is doing big business. The day is hot. Everything is all set for a perfect day at the ballpark. Everything is here, no matter what the outcome may be. The outcome of the game and the outcome of the day do not matter. Like the outcome of all things, the game and the day in Lil' Yokohama have little to do with this business of outcome. That is left for moralists to work on years later.

Meanwhile, here is the third inning. Boy, oh boy! The southpaw from San Jose, Sets Mizutani, has his old soupbone working. In three innings Alameda hasn't touched him, not even Slugger Hironaka. Along with Mizutani's airtight pitching, San Jose has managed to put across a run in the second. The San Jose fans cackle and cheer. "Atta-boy! Atta-boy!" The stands are a bustle of life, never still, noisy from by-talk and cries and the shouts and jeers and cheers from across the diamond. "Come on, Hironaka! Do your stuff!"… "Wake up, Alameda! Blast the Asahis out of the park!"… "Keep it up, Mizutani! This is your day! Tell 'em to watch the smoke go by."… "Come on, Slugger! We want a homer! We want a homer!"

It was a splendid day to be out. The sun is warm, and in the stands the clerks, the grocers, the dentists, the doctors, the florists, the lawnmower-pushers, the housekeepers, the wives, the old men sun themselves and crack peanuts. Everybody in Lil' Yokohama is out. Papa Hatanaka, the father of baseball among California Japanese, is sitting in these stands behind the backstop, in the customary white shirt—coatless, hatless, brown as chocolate and perspiring: great voice, great physique, great lover of baseball. Mrs. Horita is here, the mother of Ted Horita, the star left fielder of Alameda. Mr. and Mrs. Matsuda of Lil' Yokohama; the Tatsunos; the families of Nodas, Uyedas, Abes, Kikuchi, Yamanotos, Sasakis; Bob Fukuyama; Mike Matoi; Mr. Tanaka, of Tanaka Hotel; Jane Miyazaki; Hideo Mitoma; the Iriki sisters; Yuriko Tsudama; Suda-san, Eto-san, Higuchi-san of our block… the faces we know but not the names: the names we know and do not name.

In the seventh, Slugger Hironaka connects for a home run with two on! The Alameda fans go mad. They are still three runs behind, but what of that? The game is young; the game is theirs till the last man is out. But Mizutani is smoking them in today. Ten strike-outs to his credit already.

The big game ends, and the San Jose Asahis win. The score doesn't matter. Cheers and shouts and laughter still ring in the stands. Finally it all ends—the noise, the game, the life in the park; and the popcorn man starts his car and goes up Clement.

It is Sunday evening in Lil' Yokohama, and the late dinners commence. Someone who did not go to the game asks, "Who won today?" "San

Jose," we say. "Oh, gee," he says. "But Slugger knocked another home run," we say. "What again? He sure is good!" he says. "Big league scouts ought to size him up." "Sure," we say.

Tomorrow is a school day, tomorrow is a work day, tomorrow is another twenty-four hours. In Lil' Yokohama night is almost over. On Sunday nights the block is peaceful and quiet. At eleven thirty-six Mr. Komai dies of heart failure. For several days he has been in bed. For fourteen years he has lived on our block and done gardening work around Piedmont, Oakland, and San Leandro. His wife is left with five children. The neighbors go to the house to comfort the family and assist in the funeral preparations.

Today which is Monday the sun is bright again, but the sick cannot come out and enjoy it. Mrs. Koike is laid up with pneumonia and her friends are worried. She is well known in Lil' Yokohama.

Down the block a third-generation Japanese American is born. A boy. They name him Franklin Susumu Amano. The father does not know of the birth of his boy. He is out of town driving a truck for a grocer.

Sam Suda, who lives down the street with his mother, is opening a big fruit market in Oakland next week. For several years he has been in Los Angeles learning the ropes in the market business. Now he is ready to open one and hire a dozen or more men.

Upstairs in his little boarding room, the country boy has his paints and canvas ready before him. All his life Yukio Takaki has wanted to come to the city and become an artist. Now he is here; he lives on Seventh Street. He looks down from his window, and the vastness and complexity of life bewilder him. But he is happy. Why not? He may succeed or not in his ambition; that is not really important.

Sixteen days away, Satoru Ugaki and Tayeko Akagawa are to be married. Lil' Yokohama knows them well. Sam Suda is a good friend of Satoru Ugaki. The young Amanos know them. The Higuchis of our block are close friends of Tayeko Akagawa and her family.

Something is happening to the Etos of the block. All of a sudden they turn in their old '30 Chevrolet for a new Oldsmobile Eight! They follow this with a new living-room set and a radio and a new coat of paint for the house. On Sundays the whole family goes for an outing. Sometimes it is to Fleishhacker Pool or to Santa Cruz. It may be to

Golden Gate Park or to the ocean or to their relatives in the country.... They did not strike oil or win the sweepstakes. Nothing of the kind happens in Lil' Yokohama, though it may any day.... What then?

Today which is Tuesday Lil' Yokohama is getting ready to see Ray Tatemoto off. He is leaving for New York, for the big city, to study journalism at Columbia. Everybody says he is taking a chance going so far away from home and his folks. The air is a bit cool and cloudy. At the station Ray is nervous and grins foolishly. His friends bunch around him, shake hands, and wish him luck. This is his first trip out of the state. Now and then he looks at his watch and up and down the tracks to see if his train is coming.

When the train arrives and Ray Tatemoto is at last off for New York, we ride back on the cars to Lil' Yokohama. Well, Ray Tatemoto is gone, we say. The folks will not see him for four or six years. Perhaps never. Who can tell? We settle back in the seats and pretty soon we see the old buildings of Lil' Yokohama. We know we are home.... So it goes.

Today which is Wednesday we read in the *Mainichi News* about the big games scheduled this Sunday. The San Jose Asahis will travel to Stockton to face the Yamatos. The Stockton fans want to see the champs play once again. At Alameda, the Sacramento Mikados will cross bats with the Taiiku Kai boys.

And today which is every day the sun is out again. The housewives sit on the porch and the old men sit in the shade and read the papers. Across the yard a radio goes full blast with Benny Goodman's band. The children come back from Lincoln Grammar School. In a little while the older ones will be returning from Tech High and McClymonds High. Young boys and young girls will go down the street together. The old folks from the porches and the windows will watch them go by and shake their heads and smile.

The day is here and is Lil' Yokohama's day.

—1941

The Distant Call of the Deer

The Distant Call of the Deer

Perhaps you've heard him on one of the amateur hours around the Bay Region. If you have you will know him and all you have to do is follow what I have to say and perhaps you may add something more to the tale. If you do not know him already I must tell you. Sooner or later you will be hearing stories about him and I would like first to acquaint him to you.

Togo Satoshima is not my friend but I know him. He lives in the tankhouse back of the house which he owns. In the house he lives with his wife and five children; he eats, sleeps, and talks in the house but when he goes up to the tankhouse sometimes he forgets to come back to the house. He has a cot up there and whenever he is tired he lies down for a nap.

When Togo Satoshima is up in the tankhouse the neighbors generally know it. You couldn't be private with a pipe like his and his talent. The Japanese call the instrument shakuhachi. It is a flute-like piece of bamboo with a number of holes which your fingers fool with. And when Togo Satoshima goes up to the tankhouse and picks up the shakuhachi there is no one who can call him down. His wife gave up long ago. Recently the neighbors called a meeting to plan how they could persuade Togo Satoshima to quit his call of art. The neighbors are still wondering whether it is easier on them to muffle all the dog howls in the neighborhood when Togo begins blowing or to allow the dog and cat howls to have voice and maybe drown out the music. Meanwhile some of the folks have gone so far as to bring down from the attic the old radio earphones to protect themselves when Togo Satoshima really gets going.

No matter how many ways Togo Satoshima plays the music you will get to know he is playing "The Distant Call of the Deer." It is the only piece he knows.

Togo Satoshima has an old phonograph up in the tankhouse which you must crank to play the records. On each practice session you can hear in the beginning some master of Japan blowing a shakuhachi. That is the record playing "The Distant Call of the Deer." After several rounds of listening, Togo Satoshima accompanies him for more rounds. And when he is really warmed up Togo Satoshima begins his solos.

Soon he began to have the undivided attention of the neighborhood. People who did not trouble to know him before began to notice him.

"What is Satoshima-san up to?" someone would ask.

"He is crazy," another would answer. "Something in his head got mixed up. He is crazy."

"He's too old to go overboard like this," the third one would say. "But does he know it?"

Togo Satoshima isn't any too young to go gallivanting around and do crazy things. He is fifty-three this year and has a twenty-five-year-old daughter to think of. Togo's wife keeps nagging him about their girl. "She must have a husband real soon," she says to him. But Togo Satoshima is above petty matters. You do not know Togo until he gets inside his tankhouse.

The funny part of Togo Satoshima's drive for art is his utter lack of ambition to become professional. Perhaps he is not that far gone. But when he began to cavort around with the young people, vying for honors and prizes at the amateur hours and nights, his wife threw up her hands and went into tantrums. The neighbors stood around speechless.

It began one day when Togo Satoshima came to realize there were amateur hours and nights and there were other amateurs in this world besides himself. When he learned how big his world really was, he came into his own. That was his opinion. He became more daring and began to look about in the new big world of his.

One of his youthful friends tipped him off about radio auditions and trials on the amateur nights. When he found this new goal to work for he went more often into the tankhouse. Sometimes even in the daytime the neighbors began to hear the notes of "The Distant Call of the Deer."

There is no question that Togo Satoshima is an amazing person. I do not know how many times he did not qualify for the amateur hours. He must have had dozens of auditions with the different amateur hour programs besides the auditions for the amateur nights. Anyway, he finally got into one of the amateur hours later, which did not get him anything but a few votes.

However, when the few votes came his way, Togo Satoshima firmly believed in himself and his call of art. There was no stopping him then. After that he tried many times to qualify for the amateur hours and nights without success. When he could not get in for a long stretch of time he went out to parties and benefits and played his shakuhachi. And each time he played it was "The Distant Call of the Deer."

Meanwhile Togo Satoshima's neighborhood returned to normal. The playing of shakuhachi in the tankhouse was less heard. The neighbors began to sleep early and were undisturbed, and the dogs of the block had time to recuperate from throat troubles. His wife and children saw Togo Satoshima often in the house. Everything was back to normal but it did not last long.

I suppose the whole thing happened because Togo Satoshima was really trying all the time. When he was quiet he was not all through but was getting ready for the debut. His chance really did come weeks later when he was billed among the fourteen contestants to try for the three prizes donated by the Tsurui Jewelry Co. This particular amateur night, which was the most important event of Togo Satoshima's life, thus far, was sponsored by Asahi Athletic Club.

Out of the fourteen contestants who performed that night in the Asahi Auditorium all but Togo Satoshima were youngsters. Youngsters who were in high schools or the graduates who worked somewhere or did not have jobs. There were three contestants of grade-school ages but this did not stop Togo Satoshima from doing his best.

When the applause machine finally had done its duty for the evening, contestant number seven, which was Togo Satoshima, won third prize. By the hand clapping of the audience we could not tell who was the third prize winner but when the applause machine chose Togo Satoshima for third prize there was no end of clapping by the audience. Perhaps they were clapping for the age of the contestant number seven, not Togo

Satoshima. I do not know. Anyway, it does not matter now. No one could hold back Togo Satoshima that night. Late into the night he was still passing around cigars, jumping up and down like a kid.

Togo Satoshima is back in the tankhouse again, burning electric till wee hours in the morning, blowing his shakuhachi. Over and over the notes of "The Distant Call of the Deer" float and jar into the air and the dog howls join in unison. The neighbors' old earphones appear again. Togo Satoshima's wife holds up her hands again in despair and goes about her work in the house with the daybreak.

And with the news of Togo Satoshima's prize-winning feat the neighbors are a little more worried and the end of the tankhouse episodes is nowhere near.

—1937

The Seventh Street Philosopher

The Seventh Street Philosopher

He is what our community calls the Seventh Street philosopher. This is because Motoji Tsunoda used to live on Seventh Street sixteen or seventeen years ago and loved even then to spout philosophy and talk to the people. Today he is living on an estate of an old lady who has hired him as a launderer for a dozen years or so. Ever so often he comes out of his washroom, out of obscurity, to mingle among his people, and this is usually the beginning of something like a furore, something that upsets the community, the people, and Motoji Tsunoda alike.

There is nothing like it in our community, nothing so fruitless and irritable which lasts so long and persists in making a show; only Motoji Tsunoda is unique. Perhaps his being alone, a widower, working alone in his sad washroom in the old lady's basement and washing the stuff that drops from the chute and drying them on the line has quite a bit to do with his behavior when he meets the people of our community. Anyway, when Motoji Tsunoda comes to the town and enters into the company of the evening all his silent hours and silent vigils with deep thoughts and books come to the fore and there is no stopping of his flow of words and thoughts. Generally, the people are impolite when Motoji Tsunoda begins speaking, and the company of the evening either disperse quite early or entirely ignore his philosophical thoughts and begin conversations on business or weather or how the friends are getting along these days. And the strangeness of it all is that Motoji Tsunoda is a very quiet man, sitting quietly in the corner, listening to others talk until the opportunity comes. Then he will suddenly become alive and the subject

49

and all the subjects in the world become his and the company of the evening his audience.

When Motoji Tsunoda comes to the house he usually stays till one in the morning or longer if everybody in the family are polite about it or are sympathetic with him. Sometimes there is no subject for him to talk of, having talked himself out, but this does not slow him up. Instead he will think for a moment and then begin on his favorite topic: What is there for the individual to do today? And listening to him, watching him gesture desperately to bring over a point, I am often carried away by this meek man who launders for an old lady on weekdays. Not by his deep thoughts or crazy thoughts but by what he is and what he is actually and desperately trying to put across to the people and the world.

"Tsunoda-san, what are you going to speak on tonight?" my mother says when our family and Motoji Tsunoda settle down in the living room.

"What do you want to hear?" Motoji Tsunoda answers. "Shall it be about Shakyamuni's boyhood or shall we continue where we left off last week and talk about Dewey?"

That is a start. With the beginning of words there is no stopping of Motoji Tsunoda, there is no misery in his voice nor in his stance at the time as he would certainly possess in the old washroom. His tone perks up, his body becomes straight, and in a way this slight meek man becomes magnificent, powerful, and even inspired. He is proud of his debates with the numerous Buddhist clergymen and when he is in a fine fettle he delves into the various debates he has had in the past for the sake of his friends. And no matter what is said or what has happened in the evening, Motoji Tsunoda will finally end his oration or debate with something about the tradition and the blood flow of Shakyamuni, St. Shinran, Akegarasu, and Motoji Tsunoda. He is not joking when he says this. He is very serious. When anyone begins kidding about it, he will sadly gaze at the joker and shake his head.

About this time something happened in our town which Motoji Tsunoda to this day is very proud of. It was an event which has prolonged the life of Motoji Tsunoda, acting as a stimulant, that of broadcasting to the world in general the apology of being alive.

It began very simply, nothing of deliberation, nothing of vanity or pride, but simply the eventual event coming as the phenomenon of chance. There was the talk about this time of Akegarasu, the great phi-losopher of Japan, coming to our town to give a lecture. He, Akegarasu, was touring America, lecturing and studying and visiting Emerson's grave, so there was a good prospect of having this great philosopher come to our community and lecture. And before anyone was wise to his move, Motoji Tsunoda voluntarily wrote to Akegarasu, asking him to lecture on the night of July 14, since that was the date he had hired the hall. And before Motoji Tsunoda had received an answer he went about the town saying the great philosopher was coming, that he was coming to lecture at the hall.

He came to our house breathless with the news. Someone asked him if he had received a letter of acceptance and Akegarasu had consented to come.

"No, but he will come," Motoji Tsunoda said. "He will come and lecture. Be sure of that."

For days he went about preparing for the big reception, forgetting his laundering, forgetting his meekness, working as much as four men to get the Asahi Auditorium in shape. For days ahead he had all the chairs lined up, capable of seating five hundred people. Then the word came to him that the great philosopher was already on his way to Seattle to embark for Japan. This left Motoji Tsunoda very flat, leaving him to the mercy of the people who did not miss the opportunity to laugh and taunt him.

"What can you do?" they said and laughed. "What can you do but talk?"

Motoji Tsunoda came to the house, looking crestfallen and dull. We could not cheer him up that night; not once could we lift him from misery. But the next evening, unexpectedly, he came running in the house, his eyes shining, his whole being alive and powerful. "Do you know what?" he said to us. "I have an idea! A great idea."

So he sat down and told us that instead of wasting the beautiful hall, all decorated and cleaned and ready for five hundred people to come and sit down, he, Motoji Tsunoda would give a lecture. He said he had already phoned the two Japanese papers to play up his lecture and let the world know he would be lecturing on July 14. He said for us to be sure to come. He said he had phoned all his friends and acquaintances and reporters to be sure to come. He said he was going home now to plan his lecture, he said this was his happiest moment of his life and wondered why he did not think of giving a lecture at the Asahi Auditorium before. And as he strode off to his home and to lecture plans, for a moment I believed he had outgrown the life of a launderer, outgrown the meekness and derision, outgrown the patheticness of it and the loneliness. And seeing him stride off with unknown power and unknown energy I firmly believed Motoji Tsunoda was on his own, a philosopher by rights, as all men are in action and thought philosophers by rights.

We did not see Motoji Tsunoda for several days. However, in the afternoon of July 14 he came running up our steps. "Tonight is the big night, everybody," he said. "Be sure to be there tonight. I speak on a topic of great importance."

"What's the time?" I said.

"The lecture is at eight," he said. "Be sure to come, everybody."

The night of July 14 was like any other night, memorable, fascinating, miserable; bringing together under a single darkness, one night of performance, of patience and the impatience of the world, the bravery of a single inhabitant and the untold braveries of all the inhabitants of the earth, crying and uncrying for salvation and crying just the same; beautiful gestures and miserable gestures coming and going; and the thoughts unexpressed and the dreams pursued to be expressed.

We were first to be seated and we sat in the front. Every now and then I looked back to see if the people were coming in. At 8:10 there were six of us in the audience. Motoji Tsunoda came on the platform and sat down and when he saw us he nodded his head. He sat alone up there, he was to introduce himself.

We sat an hour or more to see if some delay had caused the people to be late. Once Motoji Tsunoda came down and walked to the entrance to see if the people were coming in. At 9:18 Motoji Tsunoda stood up and introduced himself. Counting the two babies there were eleven of us in the audience.

When he began to speak on his topic of the evening, "The Apology of Living," his voice did not quiver, though Motoji Tsunoda was unused to public speaking, and I think that was wonderful. I do not believe he was aware of his audience when he began to speak, whether it was a large audience or a small one. And I think that also was wonderful.

Motoji Tsunoda addressed the audience for three full hours without intermission. He hardly even took time out to drink a glass of water. He stood before us and, in his beautiful sad way, tried to make us understand as he understood; tried with every bit of finesse and deep thought to reveal to us the beautiful world he could see and marvel at, but which we could not see.

Then the lecture was over and Motoji Tsunoda sat down and wiped his face. It was wonderful, the spectacle; the individual standing up and expressing himself, the earth, the eternity, and the audience listening and snoring, and the beautiful auditorium standing ready to accommodate more people.

As for Motoji Tsunoda's speech, that is another matter. In a way, however, I thought he did some beautiful philosophizing that night. No matter what his words might have meant, no matter what gestures and what provoking issues he might have spoken in the past, there was this man, standing up and talking to the world, and also talking to vindicate himself to the people, trying as hard as he could so he would not be misunderstood. And as he faced the eleven people in the audience including the two babies, he did not look foolish, he was not just a bag of wind. Instead I am sure he had a reason to stand up and have courage and bravery to offset the ridicule, the nonsense, and the misunderstanding.

And as he finished his lecture there was something worthwhile for everyone to hear and see, not just for the eleven persons in the auditorium but for the people of the earth: that of his voice, his gestures, his sadness, his patheticness, his bravery, which are of common lot and something the people, the inhabitants of the earth, could understand, sympathize, and remember for a while.

—1945

The Woman Who Makes Swell Doughnuts

The Woman Who Makes Swell Doughnuts

There is nothing I like to do better than to go to her house and knock on the door and when she opens the door, to go in. It is one of the experiences I will long remember—perhaps the only immortality that I will ever be lucky to meet in my short life—and when I say experience I do not mean the actual movement, the motor of our lives. I mean by experience the dancing of emotions before our eyes and inside of us, the dance that is still but is the roar and the force capable of stirring the earth and the people.

Of course, she, the woman I visit, is old and of her youthful beauty there is little left. Her face of today is coarse with hard water and there is no question that she has lived her life: given birth to six children, worked side by side with her man for forty years, working in the fields, working in the house, caring for the grandchildren, facing the summers and winters and also the springs and autumns, running the household that is completely her little world. And when I came on the scene, when I discovered her in her little house on Seventh Street, all of her life was behind, all of her task in this world was tabbed, looked into, thoroughly attended, and all that is before her in life and the world, all that could be before her now was to sit and be served; duty done, work done, time clock punched; old-age pension or old-age security; easy chair; soft serene hours till death take her. But this was not of her, not the least bit of her.

When I visit her she takes me to the coziest chair in the living room, where are her magazines and books in Japanese and English. "Sit down," she says. "Make yourself comfortable. I will come back with some hot doughnuts just out of oil."

And before I can turn a page of a magazine she is back with a plateful of hot doughnuts. There is nothing I can do to describe her doughnuts; it is in a class by itself, without words, without demonstration. It is a doughnut, just a plain doughnut just out of oil, but it is different, unique. Perhaps when I am eating her doughnuts I am really eating her; I have this foolish notion in my head many times and whenever I catch myself doing so I say that is not so, that is not true. Her doughnuts really taste swell, she is the best cook I have ever known, Oriental dishes or American dishes.

I bow humbly that such a room, such a house exists in my neighborhood so I may dash in and out when my spirit wanes, when hell is loose. I sing gratefully that such a simple and common experience becomes an event, an event of necessity and growth. It is an event that is a part of me, an addition to the elements of the earth, water, fire, and air, and I seek the day when it will become a part of everyone.

All her friends, old and young, call her Mama. Everybody calls her Mama. That is not new, it is logical. I suppose there is in every block of every city in America a woman who can be called Mama by her friends and the strangers meeting her. This is commonplace, it is not new, and the old sentimentality may be the undoing of the moniker. But what of a woman who isn't a mama but is, and instead of priding in the expansion of her little world, takes her little circle, living out her days in the little circle, perhaps never to be exploited in a biography or on everybody's tongue, but enclosed, shut, excluded from world news and newsreels; just sitting, just moving, just alive, planting the plants in the fields, caring for the children and the grandchildren, and baking the tastiest doughnuts this side of the next world.

When I sit with her I do not need to ask deep questions, I do not need to know Plato or The Sacred Books of the East or dancing. I do not need to be on guard. But I am on guard and footloose because the room is alive.

"Where are the grandchildren?" I say. "Where are Mickey, Tadao, and Yaeko?"

"They are out in the yard," she says. "I say to them, play, play hard, go out there and play hard. You will be glad later for everything you have done with all your might."

Sometimes we sit many minutes in silence. Silence does not bother her. She says silence is the most beautiful symphony, she says the air breathed in silence is sweeter and sadder. That is about all we talk of. Sometimes I sit and gaze out the window and watch the Southern Pacific trains rumble by and the vehicles whiz with speed. And sometimes she catches me doing this and she nods her head and I know she understands that I think the silence in the room is great, and also the roar and the dust of the outside is great, and when she is nodding I understand that she is saying that this, her little room, her little circle, is a depot, a pause for the weary traveler, but outside, outside of her little world there is dissonance, hugeness of another kind, and the travel to do. So she has her little house, she bakes the grandest doughnuts, and inside of her she houses a little depot.

She is still alive, not dead in our hours, still at the old address on Seventh Street, and stopping the narrative here about her, about her most unique doughnuts, and about her personality, is the best piece of thinking I have ever done. By having her alive, by the prospect of seeing her many more times, I have many things to think and look for in the future. Most stories would end with her death, would wait till she is peacefully dead and peacefully at rest but I cannot wait that long. I think she will grow, and her hot doughnuts just out of the oil will grow with softness and touch. And I think it would be a shame to talk of her doughnuts after she is dead, after she is formless.

Instead I take today to talk of her and her wonderful doughnuts when the earth is something to her, when the people from all parts of the earth may drop in and taste the flavor, her flavor, which is everyone's and all flavor; talk to her, sit with her, and also taste the silence of her room and the silence that is herself; and finally go away to hope and keep alive what is alive in her, on earth and in men, expressly myself.

—1941

59

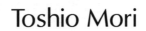

Toshio Mori

Toshio Mori

In the late afternoon he began wanting to go to the city. When the quitting time came he wanted very much to go to the city. All day the spell of bleakness and dullness witched him, and although the day was unusually warm and sunny he could not erase the spell. He wanted to do something, to do anything, to move, to get over the feeling that was disturbing him. He could think of nothing to do but go to the city, to crush and wipe out this ominous feeling of standing alone, walking alone, going alone, without a nod or a smile or caress or better, an understanding from someone.

Tonight Teruo boarded the bus, leaving behind what to him was sad and dark today, and looking forward, expectantly, hopefully, to the night and the city and the people to revive him, his spirit, and the return of undivorced feeling toward the world, the people, the life. He was certain there was that quality in the city to reward him for his efforts. He would go to the friends, go to the girls' houses, go to the spots that would bring back the old days, and go to a show if necessary, go everywhere, go to all the places and the people tonight to drown out this senseless strain and motion.

He sat, riding to the city, without a thought of the past which was this afternoon, deliberately forgetting, erasing the melancholia. Once he recalled the afternoon. "Must you go tonight?" his mother had said. "Yes, I must go tonight," he had said. "I must go no matter what else happens." And he meant it. Tonight he could not sit with the family and talk. Tonight he could not listen to the radio; he could not read. He could not, moreover, sit in silence like other nights, in constant wake of

63

himself and the field he worked in the daytime. So he was doing right tonight. Something in the city would divert his attention or someone would see and understand the state he was in and would lend a hand. Everything would come out all right, he said to himself; everything must come out all right.

Teruo got off at Twelfth and Clay and walked down a block and turned up Eleventh Street. He headed straight for Tsuyuko's home without much thought. Then, walking closer to the house that was gay and lively, he could see her sitting in the living room reading or listening to the short-wave program from Japan or playing those sad melancholy songs on the Japanese records. He could see her running up to him when the doorbell rings and crying, "Oh, hello! Teruo. How glad I am to see you!"

He was confident she was home. And nearing her home he could see the bright lighted living room and knew she was home. She would always be home. That was her nature, he thought. So when she opened the door and squealed in delight he was certain now everything would turn out right.

"Oh, hello, Teruo!" she said. "How delightful! Do come in!"

But that was not all. There were two young men in the room. He recognized one of them as Haruo Aratani and the other he did not know and Tsuyuko introduced him. They sat down and the conversation which was interrupted by his entrance was resumed. And between laughter and talk Tsuyuko asked him how he was getting along these days. He said he was just so-so.

The moment Teruo sat down he knew the place was not for him. There was the same gaiety and liveliness in the room, the same Tsuyuko of other nights, but it was not the same. As he sat in the midst of laughter and lively chatter he felt he was out of it all, alone, alien, orphaned. The contrast he was playing in the room, helplessly coming, shook him, and the longer he remained in the room, the more he thought of this and the helplessness of himself. He sat forty minutes thinking, still hoping that something might happen, that some little bit of a thing or a gesture or a movement would change the makeup of the room to something that would resurrect him but it did not come. He sat ill, stifling, wanting to move, to talk, and that something did not happen and he did not move. Teruo left early, Tsuyuko saw him off at the door and told him to come again real soon. When he crossed the street to the other side he saw Tsuyuko through the window, returning to the living room that was gaiety and laughter and two young men.

He began to walk rapidly with no mind as to where he was going. For blocks he could think of nothing else. She was not at fault. She really was herself and the two young men were blameless. There was nothing that had irritated him, no incident, no envy or jealousy to be furious about. It made him all the more sad and deserted.

Just tonight, he thought. If we had been alone together, just tonight, it might have been different. She might understand, she might only have smiled and listened and said nothing and it might have done a world of good for him. Just to have her close to him tonight, to understand him as he understood his state of feeling, would have been sufficient. That was all he would ask for. She could go with the two young men anytime, anywhere, all the other times and that was all right. She could go as she pleased and that was right. But tonight, he thought, tonight was different.

After walking blocks of city blocks he remembered the home on Sixth Street. He could go and see Yuri. He was in town; this was the time to see her. He would talk to her. She was serious and read books and she might understand. In time, by talking and listening he might find the way to the outlet and forget the emptiness of self and dullness of time. She could understand; yes, she could.

He quickened his pace. Already it was nine o'clock. He must hasten to catch Yuri home. When he knocked on the door the mother came out. She said Yuri went out early and would not be home till late but wouldn't he come in and have tea. He declined; and having left the steps and the sidewalks of her block, he turned once more toward the city.

He could think of nothing else to do. He did not feel like going to a movie now. Through his head raced a number of names that were familiar. Names of his friends, names of his parents' intimates, and special names, Bob, Tora, Kazumi, Sumio, Min, George. But the names did not come alive; he could think of nothing to do in the city, having now played his hunches and failed.

Reaching the town he went in Tabe Drug's soda fountain and sat and ordered a vanilla milkshake. Razzy, the soda jerker, remembered him and hailed. "How's the tricks?" he said. "Not so hot," Teruo said, "does the old gang still come in?" "Yes, you bet," Razzy said. "Tora, Sumio, Kazumi, Bob, Butch, Min, George." "Have they come in recently?" Teruo said. "No, not for quite a while," the soda jerker said. That was all.

While he was sipping his milkshake Sumio and his woman came in. Sumio came over and both slapped each other's back. "How's the old boy?" Sumio said. "Fine," said Teruo, "how are you?" "Great," said Sumio. They talked for a while about the old gang and the old days, and then Sumio went back to his table.

Five minutes later Teruo said goodbye and left.

He walked up Broadway toward the theatrical center thinking of going home now at 9:45. There was nothing to do but go home. All his efforts had failed, each effort making him more miserable and conscious of aloneness and sadness. He decided he might just as well go home and bury himself in the bed.

But approaching the theater, his eyes were attracted to the bright lights of its front, bright and cheery in illumination, suggesting hope and cheerfulness inside. He might as well, he thought, take a last fling for the night. So Teruo bought a ticket and went inside the Roosevelt Theater to see the vaudeville.

He remembered watching a comic with a little bit of an accordion and a big-size accordion. With the little accordion he had a trick note that made a noise like a raspberry from a human mouth. Every once in a while he would sound this note and the people laughed. He had a face like Harry Langdon or Lloyd Hamilton of the old silent pictures, looking pathetic and funny. He was trying to be funny and wasn't funny, and was funny for the lack of it. Then Teruo remembered a lovely blonde singing into the microphone in her throaty voice of being away from the Ozarks, of wanting to go back there, of seeing her pappy and the smell of chicken dinner, and of the Ozarks calling her back. It made him sad and her beautiful face and innocence made it all the more tragic and agonizing that she, with her beauty, should sing such sad songs. He could stand it no more. When the vaudeville was over he walked out of the theater, missing the double features.

When Teruo reached home the house was dark. It was dead still as if no one were occupying the house but himself coming home and occupying the place. But he knew his parents were sleeping inside and his brothers were also sleeping.

He sat on the edge of the bed, making little noise, and began undressing. He was aware that the night was almost over, that tonight was almost through with him. But he knew he was not through with the state of his feeling. Instead, tonight increased the fervor of sadness and loneliness, and for a long while Teruo did not shut off his light.

He was still up at two in the morning. He could hear the breathing of his mother sleeping in the next room, and on the other side of the wall he could hear his brother snoring. He sat, aware that no one knew him as he knew himself. He knew even Mother and his brother Hajime could not see his state of feeling; that no one in this world would see, and if seeing would not see, unable to understand and share his state of feeling that was accumulating and had been accumulating since birth.

—1940

The Chauvinist

The Chauvinist

Kettle whistles. Three pans of corn boil. Tall glasses tinkle with the touch of human hands. Plates rattle and scratch one another. An ancient refrigerator rumbles every once in a while. A clock on the wall ticks time, and he whistles a tune that was the rage a few months ago. Voices in the living room murmur like a chorus in a classical work. An electric mixer whirls. Result: mayonnaise for tuna salad. Cheese crackers crackle coming out of a two-pound carton. Knives, forks, and spoons contact the forks, spoons, and knives; and the melody of the kitchen ensues.

He's a man on Ninth Street with a great calling. A calling that may someday replace priests and theology. A calling demanding dignity, humbleness, humor, and the limits of human traits. The sadness of this particular man's role is that it must be kept a secret. He couldn't go out in the street and shout with all the might of his lungs just what he's doing as a contribution toward the harmony of human beings. He isn't looking for immortality; so he denounces personal immortality. He is looking for immortality of the man living today who is to die tomorrow. Call it as he does: everyday immortality.

Takanoshin Sakoda has been at it for a long time. In his quiet solemn way he's been searching among his friends and people for the solution to his school of thoughts. He isn't extraordinary. He isn't brilliant, and inside his head there isn't a bag full of philosophical ideas or tricks. There isn't a particle of outstanding skill in him which may be the undoing of his calling. There is just one thing which sets him apart from the rest of men and that's the story herein.

People look and size him up: when he talks he is like a swirling river seeking an ocean outlet. He won't hear other people's words. He just goes on talking. He forgets the people, the background, and even himself to the point of nothingness in a subject of temporary importance.

Friends look at him from another angle: lucky guy. Stone deaf. Doesn't have to plug cotton in his ears when to bed he goes with little wifey. Doesn't need to pick up little issues of a family circle. The innocent among the snoopy gossipers and savages of dirty insults. The babe in the gusty screechy roar of modern mads—the genius of the community due to an accidental lack of a sense.

The family in one voice (wife, daughter, and son): the blessed wit. One-half of a battleless ground. The desert of mind, culture, age, and ambition. The portrait of a man in a thousand years: a "house-band"— the meek follower of a new suffrage for power (now) and beauty (in future). The seed of a new vogue: the specialist specializing with a lack of one human sense or more. Examples of possibilities: the blind artist painting on the accepted presence of a canvas; the deaf musician composing a fresh score—new tones, new scales, new instruments; the tongueless chef concocting a new dish fit for a connoisseur; the mouthless moralist discovering in silence the language of expression; the average man on earth smelling the presence of man on Mars.

Today is the day. Takanoshin is sitting in the kitchen having finished his duties early. Everything's cooked; everything's on the table ready to be guzzled by the ladies. The women arrive. It's seven in the evening, and his wife hasn't returned. Business must've been good. Good business on Monday. Monday is Community Women's Club night.

Mrs. Tamada is looking at him and addressing Mrs. Abe. "Sometimes I believe he can hear us," she is saying. "Sometimes I see an intelligent look on his face as if he knows everything that's going on."

"Nonsense!" Mrs. Abe replies. "Look at him! Unless he's a good actor, and I know he isn't, he couldn't stare at us so long with that empty blandness of his without being genuine."

Mrs. Tamada is dubious of her companion's words. "Sometimes I feel he's laughing at us."

"Here, here! What's all this debating about?" Mrs. Tariki cuts in.

Mrs. Tamada and Mrs. Abe turn their backs on Takanoshin. "We're talking about Takanoshin. Tamada-san says he's very intelligent and can see through us," Mrs. Abe says.

"I did not!" Mrs. Tamada says.

Mrs. Tariki laughs. It's time to put everyone in place. It's about time someone definitely defined the activity of Takanoshin. "Picture him sitting there night after night waiting for his wife and worrying about supper getting cold," she says. "Picture him with an apron housecleaning twice a week while his wife and daughter run the grocery store."

"He's lazy, weak, and boneless," Mrs. Abe says.

"He should be ashamed of himself staying home by the warm stove while his wife is working at the store," adds Mrs. Tamada.

The fourth woman enters the conversation. "The weasel. The tramp. The mind of a monkey," Mrs. Miyakawa says. "Good for nothing."

The four women turn and look in Takanoshin's direction.

He is nonchalantly sitting in the corner, the way immobile and wise people do. He meets their glances with a smile, the way the tolerant sages of history should have done. He is all smiles because he could not have heard the conversation. He is deaf. His ears are out of order. He looks at the ceiling and smiles. Everything is out of order. The arrangement of his life for instance is out of order. The women are out of order; his family is out of order. The system of civilization is out of order. Ditto the people and the world.

Out of his isolation in the kitchen (cooking three meals a day is his relation to the labor problem today) he has discovered one of the biggest scoops of scientific nature. It took him eighty days and nights to see the light that one of the biggest things out of order on earth is the facts misarranged. The facts of life are; the past thus, the future thus. Proven with dignity and pomp; prophesied with sanity and bearing it is to laugh. Tonight two stars have fallen. I saw two of them fall while I was outdoors for a bit of night air. That's the fact of life for today and another day. It was time that one man on Eighth Street in the year 1939 come to grief. It was once simple to prove the fact of an event. The world in general is concerned over me because I am deaf. Even at this moment when I am sitting here peacefully and listening to the conversation as sanely and conscious as the women themselves, I am proof of the deaf living.

73

I the man who remains silent to the little voices about me. I did not declare myself to be anything. I am one of the living proofs of a fact purported to life. One day I simply sat down, and the family began to screech at me. It took them ten minutes to come to my side and look at each other's faces. "He can't hear," my son hoarsely whispers. "He's gone deaf!" my daughter screams. My wife pales and begins to sway and the children rush her to the sofa. Commotion arose. People came in and out. Doctors looked over me. I became the attraction of the community.

Although the news of myself being deaf became old and died, I myself knew no better than to become the beginning of a new refreshment of life. I endorse myself, my life, to the young mind—not for mischief and troublemaking. I address to the suppressed, the futile, the jobless, the woman's husband, the lonely hearts. I also address the romanticist—here is something in your line. I am deaf. This is untruth but I'm not lying. A liar is a cheat who harms others. I am like a beggar who must become blind to make a living. The only difference is that I have become deaf to survive the living. The world is waiting for a new philosophy. This is the age for science and invention. People deride the experimenters' failures but we need the experimenters and the failures. We need them just as we need the untruths. Truth without untruth, it's false. By representing the truth in untruth and untruth in truth I may become someone I want to be.

Mrs. Sakoda returns home. The women stand. The meeting begins right away. Tonight is the flower arrangement night. Refreshments are served. Mrs. Sakoda is speaking, "My, he's ruined the punch again!"

"Mama! Will you taste the salad? It's salty!" the daughter calls from the next room.

The women look at Takanoshin sitting in the adjoining room and laugh. They laugh heartily and the words are heard through the house.

"I'm sorry, girls," Mrs. Sakoda is speaking again. "The evening's spoiled again. I've told him over and over and he comes right back and does the same thing again."

Pretty soon their men will be coming around to take them home. They will park their cars at the front and blow their horn. The women run out to the door and call them in. The coffee is served. The conversation is now general. The men talk of business and fishing and club activities. The art of flower arrangement is over. With the entry of each man, the men perk up and smile. The weather is fine these days. Business is good. How's yours? My car goes sixteen miles on a gallon. I caught a fifteen pounder. A striped bass near Antioch. My luck's been bad. A cop pinched me in the city. Yeah, a fine. My house needs painting. Business is so bad I put it off every year. Why don't you run up to my brother's place in San Jose? He'll be glad to see you after all these years. Why don't you? Thanks. I don't know. Oh, go ahead.

Do these men talk this way away from here? Do they in their privacy speak in such a milky language? I wonder if their thoughts run parallel to the mere words of their lips. I wonder if they are dead so soon. They talk in the same tone, same gestures, same subject, same hobbies, same duties and obligations, same destiny. Why doesn't someone talk about death (slow death) some night? The death in the flower arrangement. The death in the flower. The death in our life. The death of a birth. Some people wouldn't glibly talk; it would take their minds off talk. And the silence would be refreshing and strange. Imagine the silence at the women's club meeting. The silence in a deaf man's house. The silence wouldn't be eternal; make no mistake about that. It wouldn't be what we would like to have but ah, what is eternal? And at this moment the records of Beethoven, Sibelius, Ravel, Gershwin stop. The great poems end, Shakespeare included. The books of Tolstoy, Joyce, Whitman, Emerson, Tagore; and what have you left?

I would sit for an answer by the shore and watch the waves come in. I would lie on the hills and watch the sun for a while. The clouds a good deal longer. I would go to the riverside and watch the boats sail the waters; the trains dash by; the airliners roar overhead.

It isn't there, an early observer tells the younger generation. It isn't there. Look somewhere else. At last the young generation claim. It isn't here. It isn't nature. It isn't man's civilization or man's heredity or his environment. It isn't man's possessions or capabilities, the younger generation point. It's his possibilities that count. It's a shame to see the simplicity of each generation. This is so, that is so, all is so. The man's thoughts are the seeds of the future. The last region of man is sleep, next to nothingness. The sleep of man awake. The sleep of man sleeping.

The sleep of man dreaming. The sleep of man dead. The sleep of man in birth.

The night is over. The women leave. The men follow. Goodbye, Abe-san. Goodnight, Tamada-san. Goodnight, Miyakawa, Yamamoto, Hama, Suzuki. See you next Monday. Tea ceremony next time. Oh, let's drag Karita-san next time. Smiles. More smiles. Handshakes. Hand waves. Brave smiles. Sad faces at departure.

The night is over for them. The night is dead. And sleep is a period between sunset and sunrise. The saddest of faces is the man or woman too lonely to be alone. The loneliest hour is the time before sleep and the awakening of conscious motor after sleep.

A man's loneliness is an offshoot of the women's club meeting every Monday night. The crowd which the theaters draw isn't due to the attraction of the picture or the stars, but the vacuum emptiness in each individual's search for the solace. A song like "Donkey Serenade" takes hold of the audience. It is trivial and full of death, but we are impressed temporarily. Everything we touch is full of death and triviality.

And when we sense something like a poem or a symphony or a painting that would not die we are surprised. It makes us forget temporarily by reaching out for something permanent and enduring. And often when we return to ourselves our life is like the song "Donkey Serenade" (full of death and short life)—the actuality of our faces, our houses, our cars, our relatives, our bank accounts.

"Papa-san! Papa-san!"

Across the hall the daughter calls loudly. It is time for bed. Mama-san is upstairs in bed. The kitchen light is off; so is the dining room. The clock is a tattler. The time of man is just beginning; the theme a helplessness; action the seeds of tomorrow.

I want to talk to someone. I want to talk and listen and answer. I want to sing in a chorus in tune with the rest of the crowd. I too want to join and laugh and joke. I want sometimes to tell all the people what I know and how little I know.

I cannot flee the people's world. I am more like an inarticulate person than anyone else; the indignation for want of expression to be ignited in some little source: insignificant, impotent, a dud.

Did you note one day the sun was thus and later returned to gaze again and it was thus, but you know all was changed, the sun, the earth, yourself, the nations, the oceans.

One minute you were always light-hearted and wise-cracking. You had the sense of hearing and your friends acknowledging it. You laughed your way out of difficulties, making a lark of life. You heard laughter and you laughed. Friends came around and slapped your back. Words came easy. Gestures came abruptly in childish natural movements. And in the turn of a minute you had dignity you never knew you possessed. You never lost your sense of hearing, but a day of a joke on your wife and family and friends turned the spring.

You were you yesterday. You are you today. You sit in a hole you made yourself. You sit and grin privately. You put one over. It is fun to separate for a while from your family and friends, and descend or ascend in a different role. It's all right if you are a movie actor, dropping one role and taking up another. Unless you're an actor such a holiday is difficult on earth. You must drop one role or the other. This is the saddest thing on earth because we are all actors in our poor-lit stages, unsung, unheralded, pitied for the sake of our characters and not for our roles. One minute we are a dreamer, another minute a comic, another time a banker, a poet, a statesman, a gambler, a philanthropist, a drunk, a reverend, a murderer. All this is possible to attain in a single day. We turn and twist at a moment's mood, and the force of our surroundings is mirrored in the roles.

Did you ever have a time when you'd sit in a dark room and know every man in the world? Did you remember the time you'd have such a feeling? Was it when you were happy in a revelry or when you were alone and realized your friends had stayed away very long and you did not go out and seek them?

I sat in the kitchen and watched the women come and go. I sat in the living room among my men friends and watched them. There's really nothing to report and everything to understand. Often friendship is a fog and often you will know total strangers more intimately. I found this out in the park where I go almost daily. A warm afternoon in the park among total strangers is a lift. You talk and you are free.

I sat among my people in the living room without talk; and as I sat there without laughter, just smiling, I knew they were assembled there without laughter. I remember the way they sat around and talked. I knew they were laughing at times and were without real laughter and were feverishly together for a real one.

It was on a sunny morning three hours before noon when I had walked for seven blocks and had come to a park. It was a park I had never seen before. It was the beginning of a fresh idea and the resurrection of myself; the park life of this particular park and the parks of other American cities and Berlin, London, Tokyo, Moscow, Paris, Rome were no different; and the park life and the living room life and the dark room life were all the same dough; and laughter or no laughter was the same; and death or deathless was alike; and a joke or a tragedy was out of the same stem; and the man the same.

I sat and talked with a man who came from the Oklahoma fields. I saw him but once. He never mentioned that he was of the dust bowl clan once but it was printed all over him. A man who came from Indiana talked one day for hours. He said he once worked in a nursery where he hauled the soil in a wheelbarrow. A grocer sat beside me and talked of the business conditions. A young idealist rabidly sought me for a follower. One day there was a retired capitalist sitting and talking a few seats from me, and he looked the same as anyone else. I completely lost time that day and overlooked lunch and was late cooking supper. My wife gave me hell.

Turn the disk of the earth: a bed is soaring. The clouds roar. The rivers dry. The skies drop. The sun melts. The man is bigger than the earth. Why? A dream is a better production than Warner Brothers pictures. A dream is the reality in hope; and reality the nightmare of a dream reversed. Destruction and education hand in hand. Red Cross and butchery on the same fields. Death and birth in Ward E. Asylum and earth together: fences. Barefoot and shoes, and nudism and morality. One man and one woman. One man and two women. One woman and two men. One man and many women. One woman and many men. The impatience of man. The patience of man. He sleeps. He wakes. The sleep of a man and the disk of earth continues.

Through the cracks of a cream shade the light pours in the room. The birds sing and the milk trucks rumble by. The sun is up and the room is cold. Jetliners fly; the trains whistle; the shouts of the neighbors recall the earth; the consciousness of mind awakens the presence of being.

It is morning and man is no different; the philosophy of man no different; his responsibilities are no different, his roles unchanged, and his fantasies descending. The man in bed blinks his eyes, and the rivers roll, gas and electric is on, the clock ticks, the clothes are pressed, the shoes need mending, the breakfast to make for four, the furniture to be dusted, and a park stroll scheduled.

Darkness is over, the black is gray, prison gray, and a brighter hue is present at last. And a man accepts his affliction: senseless vacuum with the waves of the earth in motion. Motionless, his nerves unflinching he attempts communication. (Wife! Son! Daughter! Wake up... new morning!) End of a man of no senses: Now not only deaf but visionless, dumb, feelingless, colorless, numb... only a sixth sense serenity. Smile, rejoice: I was once here. Soon not a trace of my presence would remain. But who cares? (I care, says the government. I care, says the church. I do, say the friends.) I second the motion... while I am still alive. While I am alive, I shall smile and laugh, and in spirit grab the grits of life, scraping for crumbs while cooking up the great feast of life.

—1935

The Trees

The Trees

"Good morning, Hashimoto, good morning," Fukushima said to his friend.

"Ah, Fukushima, what do you want?" Hashimoto said.

Fukushima rubbed his hands and stomped his feet. "It is cold. The sun is not warm enough."

Hashimoto laughed. "You are usually asleep at this time," he said. "What do you want at this early hour?"

"I came to see you and the pine trees," Fukushima said. "Do you not walk among your trees every morning?"

"Yes, you know that," said Hashimoto.

"Did you already take a walk this morning? I want to walk with you among your pine trees," said Fukushima.

"No, not yet," Hashimoto said, looking curiously. "I am going to my garden now. Come on, friend."

The two walked to the rear of the house. The sun climbed higher and the garden became warm. They walked among the pine trees. They crossed many times the little stream running alongside the path. The sparrows chattered noisily overhead. The two circled the garden several times. Then they went up and down many times, crisscrossed, and finally sat down to rest on an old stone bench.

"Hashimoto, I am your old-time friend," Fukushima said. "What do you see in the trees?"

Hashimoto looked sharply at his friend. "Why, I see the trees," he said a moment later.

"No, I do not mean it that way," Fukushima said. "That is a common expression. I want you to tell me how you really see these pine trees."

Hashimoto laughed.

"Please. I am your friend," Fukushima said. "Please tell me your secret of happiness."

"Fukushima, there is really nothing in it. I simply see the trees. That is all."

"No, that is not all. Why, anyone could see the trees," Fukushima said.

"They could and should," Hashimoto agreed.

"I came here early to see the trees. I have walked with you among the trees, and still I don't see anything in the trees. Why is that?" asked Fukushima.

The two friends looked silently at each other.

"Did you not say you were cold a few minutes ago?" Hashimoto said.

"Yes, I was cold," Fukushima admitted.

"Look at yourself now," Hashimoto said. "You are warm and perspiring. You are very warm."

"What of it? That is a fact," said Fukushima. "What are you talking about?"

"The difference between warmth and cold is movement," said Hashimoto. "And movement makes warmth and cold."

"Hashimoto, I do not want to hear about warmth and cold," pleaded Fukushima. "I want to share your happiness. I want you to explain the trees you see."

"I cannot explain the trees, Fukushima," Hashimoto said. "But listen, friend. The warmth and cold I talk about is in the trees."

Fukushima shook his head. "You are not my friend. You do not want to tell me your secret."

Hashimoto shook his head. "You are my friend, and the secret you mention is the most exposed of all."

Fukushima looked coldly at Hashimoto. "If you do not tell me your secret we shall be friends no more. You know what happened to me. A year ago I was fairly rich. I owned stocks and properties. And then fate overtook me and I lost all. I am a defeated man but I want to fight on, and I came to you."

Hashimoto nodded. "Let us try again. You were cold when you came here, but when you walked about the garden you became warm and experienced warmth. Do you see, Fukushima? You would not have known warmth if you did not walk?"

"But the trees—people tell me you have your trees, and that is why you are happy," Fukushima said.

Hashimoto shook his head sadly. His eyes roamed about the garden.

"Why are you so happy?" asked Fukushima.

"I am not always happy," cried Hashimoto. "I am cold and warm too."

"Our age is unkind to men," Fukushima said bitterly. "And you do not help a friend."

"I have tried my best," Hashimoto said.

"Some day you will see me join our friend Makino. I will join him at the crazy hospital in Stockton. He reads many books like you but he went crazy," Fukushima said.

The two looked at each other silently.

"Hashimoto, when I leave here today I shall never see you again. Please, tell me," begged Fukushima.

Hashimoto looked up eagerly. "All right, listen. You were cold when you came here, but when you walked about…"

"I do not want to hear any more!" cried Fukushima, leaping furiously to his feet. "If you cannot tell me about the trees do not talk!"

"Fukushima," cried Hashimoto. "Fukushima!"

He stood by the old stone bench and watched his friend go out the gate and into the highway.

—1942

The Chessmen

The Chessmen

Perhaps I would have heard the news in time, but if I hadn't met the third party of the three principals at the beginning it wouldn't have been the same to me. By luck that day, while I was leaning on the fence resting after a hot day's work, a young Japanese came up to me. "Hello. Where's Hatayama's nursery?" he asked me. "I was told the place was somewhere around here."

"It's half a mile farther down," I said. I pointed out the road and told him to go until he reached the greenhouses. That was Hatayama Nursery. The young Japanese thanked me and went away.

At Hatayama Nursery I knew two men, Hatayama-san and Nakagawa-san. They were the only men there the year around. The boss and his help. The two managed the three greenhouses of carnations quite capably. Only in the summer months when the carnation boxes must be lined up and filled with new soil and the plants for the next year planted, Hatayama-san hired additional men. Hatayama-Nakagawa combination worked beautifully. For seven years the two men never quarreled and seldom argued with each other. While Hatayama-san was at the flower market selling flowers to the florists, Nakagawa-san carried on at the nursery. He was wise on everything. He attended the boiler, watered the plants, made cuttings, cut flowers, and tackled the rest of the nursery work.

Every once in a while I used to visit the place and talk to these middle-aged men. Perhaps Nakagawa-san was older than his boss. I don't know. "Listen to him, Takeo," Hatayama-san used to tell me. "If you want to become a good carnation grower listen to this man. He's got something.

89

He has many years of experience and a young man like you will learn plenty by listening to him."

Nakagawa-san used to smile with these words. He talked very little. "I don't know much," he would say. "I know very little."

One of the strange things about Nakagawa-san was his family life. I used to visit him only on the weekdays. On Saturday nights and Sundays he was in Oakland to see his family. I used to wonder how he could stand it. His wife and three grown children lived in the city while he worked alone in the nursery. He made his bed, washed his work clothes, swept and mopped his bunkhouse after work hours. The only domestic work he didn't do was cook. He ate with the Hatayamas.

When I'd sit and talk with him he'd talk about his family and his weekend visits.

"My youngest boy is now out of high school," he would tell me. "He's a smart boy but I can't send him to college."

"That's too bad for him," I would say. "But you're sending Tom to Cal. That's plenty."

"Yes," he would proudly say. "I hope he'll amount to something."

Nakagawa-san's only daughter worked as a domestic in an American home and helped with the upkeep of her parents' home. Often he would tell me of his children and his eyes would shine with a faraway look.

"Why don't you stay with the family all the time, Nakagawa-san?" I'd ask him. "Why can't you get a job in Oakland and live with your family?"

He would smile. "Ah, I wish I could," he'd say. "But what could an old nursery worker do in a city? I'm too old to find other jobs. No, I must remain here."

"It's a shame," I'd tell him.

"I guess we can't have everything," he'd say and smile. "I'm lucky to have this job so long."

Several weeks after the young man had asked about Hatayama Nursery he came to see me one night. He said his name was George Murai. "I get very lonely here," he explained to me. "I never knew a nursery could be so lonely."

"You're from the city, aren't you?" I asked.

"Oakland," he said.

He was a pleasant fellow. He talked a lot and was eager. "Whenever I have the time I'm going to drop in and see you. That's if you don't mind," he said. "Over at Hatayama's I don't see any young people. I'll go crazy if I don't see somebody. In Oakland I have lots of friends."

I brought out beer and shredded shrimp. George could take beer.

"How do you like the work?" I asked him.

"Fine," he said. "I like it. Someday I'd like to have a nursery of my own. Only I hope I get over being lonely."

"You'll be all right after you get used to it," I said.

"If I don't give up at the start I'll be all right," George said. "I don't think I'll quit. I have a girl, you see."

He pulled out of his wallet a candid shot of a young girl. "That's Lorraine Sakoda of Berkeley," he said. "Do you know her?"

I shook my head.

"We're crazy about each other," George said. "As soon as I find a steady job we're going to get married."

Before the evening was over I knew George pretty well. Several times when we mentioned friends we found them mutual. That made us feel pretty good.

After the first visit George Murai came often. He would tell me how the work progressed at Hatayama Nursery. It was getting busy. The carnation boxes had to be laid out evenly on the tracks. The soil had to be worked and shoveled in. The little carnation plants must be transplanted from the ground to the boxes. It was interesting to George.

"I'm learning everything, Takeo," he said. "Some day I'll get a nursery for myself and Lorraine."

When I went over to Hatayama's to see the boss as well as Nakagawa-san and George Murai, I would catch a glimpse of a new liveliness on the place. The eagerness of George Murai was something of a charm to watch. He would trot from one task to another as if he were eagerly playing a game. His shouts and laughter filled the nursery and the two men whose capering days were over would look at each other and smile. George's singing ability pleased Hatayama-san. After supper he'd ask George to sing. George knew only the modern popular songs.

Sometimes Nakagawa-san, George, and I got together in the little house. Nakagawa-san shared the place with George. At such times George would ask question after question about carnation growing. He would ask how to get rid of red spiders; how such things as rust and spots, the menaces of the plants, could be controlled. He would press for an answer on how to take the crops at a specific period, how to avoid stem rot and root rot, what fertilizers to mix, how to take care of the cuttings. I would sit aside and listen to Nakagawa-san answer each problem patiently and thoroughly.

Sometimes the talk swung to Oakland. The three of us were attached to Oakland one way or another.

"I know your son Tom pretty well," George Murai told Nakagawa-san one night.

"Do you? Do you know Tom?" Nakagawa-san asked eagerly.

"Sure. Tom and I used to go to Tech High together," George said. "He's going to college now."

"Sure! Sure!" Nakagawa-san said.

"I know your daughter Haruyo," George said. "But I don't know Tetsuo so well."

Nakagawa-san nodded his head vigorously. "He's a smart boy but I can't send him to college like Tom."

It wasn't until I was alone with Hatayama-san one day that I began to see a change on the place. In the latter part of August Hatayama-san was usually busy hunting around for two husky men to work on the boxes. It was the time when the old plants in the greenhouses were rooted out and the boxes filled with the old soil hauled away. Then the boxes with the new carnation plants were to be hauled in. It was the beginning of heavy work in a nursery.

This year Hatayama-san said, "I can't afford to hire more men. Flower business has been bad. We'll have no flowers to sell until November. That's a long way off. After the new boxes are in I'll have to lay off the Murai boy."

"Who's going to work the boxes this year?" I asked.

"Murai and Nakagawa," Hatayama-san said. "They'll have to do it."

When the heavy work at Hatayama Nursery actually started George Murai stopped coming to see me. One afternoon when I got off early and went over there they were still out on the field. It was then I saw the struggle that knew no friendship, the deep stamp of self-preservation in human nature. Here was no flowery gesture; here were no words.

I stood and watched Nakagawa-san and George Murai push the truck-loads of carnation boxes one after another without resting. In the late afternoon their sweat dried and the cool wind made the going easier. It was obvious that George, being young and strong, could hold a stiff pace; and that he was aware that he would be laid off when the heavy work was finished. With the last opportunity to impress the boss George did his stuff.

I was certain that Nakagawa-san sensed the young man's purpose. He stuck grimly to the pace. All this was old stuff to him. He had been through it many times. Two men were needed to lift the boxes with the old soil and toss it deftly onto the pile so that no clump of dirt would be left sticking to the boxes. Two men were needed to carefully lift the boxes with the new plants and haul them into the greenhouses. The pace which one of the men worked up could show up the weaker and the slower partner. A man could break another man with a burst of speed maintained for several days. One would be certain to break down first. When a young man set up a fast pace and held it day after day it was something for a middle-aged man to think about.

Nakagawa-san straightened as if his back ached but he was trying to conceal it. His forearms must have been shot with needle-like pains but he worked silently.

As I watched Nakagawa-san and George Murai heaving and pushing with all their might I lost sight of the fact that they were the friends I knew. They were like strangers on a lonely road coming face to face with fear. They looked like men with no personal lives; no interests in family life, in Oakland, in Lorraine Sakoda, in the art of plant-growing, in friendship. But there it was in front of my eyes.

I turned back and went home. I wondered how they could share the little shack after what was happening on the field.

I went over several times but each night they were so worn out with the strain of their pace they slept early. I saw them less and less. Their house was often dark and I knew they were asleep. I would then go over to see Hatayama-san.

"Come in, come in," he would greet me.

By the manner in which he talked about Nakagawa-san and George it was plain that he too had seen the struggle on the field. He would tell me how strong and fast George was. At the rate they were going they would be finished a week ahead of the last year's schedule.

"Nakagawa is getting old," he would tell me of his friend. "He's getting too old for a worker."

"He's experienced," I would reply.

"Yes," he'd say, "but George is learning fast. Already he knows very much. He's been reading about the modern method of plant growing. I've already put in an electric hotbed through George's suggestion."

Then I knew George Murai was not so close to being fired. "Are you going to keep both of them this winter?" I asked.

Hatayama-san shook his head. "No. Can't afford it. I've got to let one of them go."

Several nights later I saw lights in their little shack and went over. George was up. He was at the sink filling the kettle with water. Nakagawa-san was in bed.

"What's happened, George?" I said. "Is Nakagawa-san sick?"

"No," George said. "He's just tired. His back aches so I'm warming it with hot water and mustard."

"I'll be all right tomorrow," Nakagawa-san said.

"You're working too hard these days, Nakagawa-san," I said. "You're straining yourself."

Nakagawa-san and George were silent. They looked at me as if I had accused them in one way or another.

Soon Nakagawa-san was back on the field. However, when I went to see how he was getting along I saw Hatayama-san out on the field with George. By the time I reached them they had pushed the truckloads of carnation boxes in and out of the greenhouses several times. George whistled when he saw me. Hatayama-san nodded his head and grinned. Something had happened to Nakagawa-san.

"I knew it was going to happen," Hatayama-san told me. "Nakagawa's getting too old for nursery work. His back troubles him again."

In the morning Nakagawa-san had stuck grimly to the work. At noon when he sat down for lunch he couldn't get up afterwards. He had to be carried to the little shack. Mrs. Hatayama applied a new plaster to his back.

"I've been on the job for two days. We'll finish on time," Hatayama-san said. "George's been a big help to me."

George looked at me and grinned.

When the pair resumed carting the boxes I went to see Nakagawa-san. As I entered the room he opened his eyes and smiled at me. He looked very tired. His repeated attempts to smile reminded me of his family and his pride for his sons.

"I'll be all right in a few days," he said eagerly. "When my back's healed I'll be like new again."

"Sure," I said. "You'll be all right."

He read to me a letter from his wife. It was filled with domestic details and his boys' activities at school. They wanted to see him soon. They missed him over the weekend. They reasoned it was due to the work at the place. They missed the money too. They wanted him to be sure and bring the money for the house rent and the gas bill.

When I came away in the late afternoon Hatayama-san and George were washing their faces and hands back of the woodshed.

"How's he getting along?" Hatayama-san asked me.

"He says he's all right," I said.

"I'll go and see if he wants anything before I eat," George said.

George trotted off to the little shack. Hatayama-san motioned me toward the house. "At the end of this month I'm going to drop Nakagawa. I hate to see him go but I must do it," he said. "Nursery is too much for him now. I hate to see him go."

"Are you really going to let him go?" I asked.

"I'm serious. He goes." He took my arm and we went inside the house. I stayed for dinner. During the courses George talked. "Someday I want to bring my girl here and introduce her," he told Hatayama-san and me. "You'll both like her."

Hatayama-san chuckled. "When will you get married, my boy?"

George smiled. "I think I can get married right away," he said.

Afterwards we listened to a few Japanese records. George got out Guy Lombardo's records and we listened to them. Mrs. Hatayama brought hot tea and Japanese teacakes. When I left George accompanied me to the road. He was in a merry mood. He whistled "I Can't Give You Any-thing But Love."

We said, "So long."

"Be sure to come again," he said. As I walked down the road I heard his whistling for quite a distance. When the whistling stopped the chants of the crickets in the fields became loud. Across the lot from the green-houses I saw the little shack lit by a single light, and I knew that Nakagawa-san was not yet asleep.

1941

The Sweet Potato

The Sweet Potato

It was the last day at Treasure Island and Hiro took me around for a last look. Time after time he shook his head as he fondly gazed at the buildings. The lights were going out at midnight.

"Gee, it gets me," he said, his eyes becoming red. "I don't like it."

All summer we had gone to the fair together. There were days when I would rather have stayed at home, but Hiro would come and pull me out of the house.

"I'm sick. I want companionship. Please come with me and make me happy," he would beg.

Each time it ended the same way. We would walk for miles, and he would talk. We saw very little of the exhibits. When we became tired we would go up on the Temple Compound and rest. Each time we would look below and watch the crowd coming and going. And each time Hiro would comment, "Gee, look at those people going back and forth. Wandering forever... that's what we're all doing. Searching for something, searching for the real thing... every one of us. Look at them going in circles. That's us when we go below and join them."

I knew what was coming next. All summer we had argued about ourselves... the problem of the second generation of Japanese ancestry. "I tell you. We're not getting anywhere. We haven't a chance," he would tell me. "We'll fall into our parents' routine life and end there. We'll have our own clique and never get out of it."

"You're wrong, Hiro," I would say. "We'll climb and make ourselves heard. We have something in us to express and we will be heard."

Hiro would shake his head. "You write stories and sing in the clouds. You dream too much."

Over and over we would talk and disagree. Whenever the situation became unpleasant we would become silent and walk. After a time the holiday spirit of the island would take hold of us and we would become lively again.

"It's this friendly spirit around here I like," I would tell him. "I hope it never fades."

"Same here," he would agree. "But the fair will be over and there'll be no more. Let's go and see the Cavalcade once more."

On the last day at the fair we walked much and said little. Our legs were aching but we did not rest. Hiro was almost crying. "Here's this wonderful thing called the fair ending tonight, definitely at midnight. The place where people came to forget awhile and laugh and sing. To-morrow the island will be empty and dark." I said nothing.

"What do you think?" he asked me suddenly. "Do you think our people will ever be noticed favorably? What can we Japanese do? Must we ac-complish big things here in America?"

"Little things can accomplish big things too, I think," I said.

"That's right," he agreed. "But it's so slow. It takes time."

At three in the afternoon we became hungry. All the eating places were filled and we had to hunt around for a place to eat. "Let's go to the Japanese Tearoom today," Hiro suggested. "We might find a table there." I agreed.

The place was filled and we had to wait for a table but we finally got one. All about us were the white people munching teacakes, sipping Japan tea, and tasting green tea ice cream. Hiro's face reddened a bit. Long secluded in the Japanese community, he looked shy and awkward. But it did not last long.

An old white lady and a young man came over to the table and asked if we would share the table with them. We readily consented. Suddenly, the old lady began to speak in Japanese.

"How are you?" she said. "Isn't it a wonderful afternoon?"

"You speak Japanese," I said, amazed.

"A little," she explained in Japanese. "I was in Japan for several years. I was in Yokohama during the big earthquake."

The young man spoke in English. "My mother and I love Japan. Have you ever been there?"

Hiro and I shook our heads. "No. We'd like to some day."

"You should visit Japan. It's a beautiful country," the young man said.

The old lady continued in Japanese. "I taught in the grade school for five years. When the earthquake came we lost everything. Fortunately my family came out alive."

"I was small then," the son said. "One day the houses were all standing in Yokohama and the next day there was nothing. It happened very quickly."

"It must've been terrible," Hiro said. "I guess there was food shortage."

"Yes, there was food shortage." The old lady nodded her head. "There wasn't enough food to go around. Do you know? There was one experience I'll always remember."

"She likes to tell it to everybody," the son said, smiling. "I remember."

"We were without food on the first day," she continued. "Nobody had food. A Japanese family whom we did not know found a single sweet potato. There were four in their family but the father cut the potato in eight parts and gave each of us a cube. The four in our family were never more filled. I cannot forget it. And afterwards a boy came along with a cupful of sterilized water and we shared that too."

"That potato was really sweet," the son said.

We nodded and said nothing. Hiro's eyes twinkled, looking first at the old lady and her son and then me. "Where do you live now?" he asked the young man.

"In Sacramento," replied the young man. "We come to San Francisco often. And whenever we do we feast on Japanese food."

"I like daikon, miso, tofu, tempura, and things cooked with shoyu," the old lady said.

"And mochi," added the young man. The old lady laughed. "My boy likes rice cake best."

"Do you like raw fish?" I asked them.

"Very much, with mustard and shoyu," was the young man's reply. "There's one thing I don't go for."

"That's the octopus," the old lady said. "It's like rubber and there's no taste."

"Say, what's going to happen to the Japanese Pavilion?" The young man suddenly changed the subject. I said it probably would be torn down.

"That's a shame." He shook his head sadly. "A beautiful building like this."

"This is a beautiful day," said the old lady. "Warm and serene. A beautiful setting for the last day."

"It certainly is," I agreed.

Hiro beamed and looked gaily about, forgetting time and place. The four of us sat there a long time as if we had known one another a good many years. The people looked curiously at us, wondering what we had in common.

—1941

The Garden

The Garden

Every now and then Tom Yamashita got up from his chair and looked out of the window to see if it was still raining. Each time, noting the heavy downpour, he paused by the window and clucked his tongue. "Why must it rain? It shouldn't rain. I have plenty of work piled up now. Why don't things go smoothly for me?" he cried time and again.

His father's friend, Papa Harada, chuckled and slowly shook his head. "The weather, career, the world... all the same. It is one matter. Sometimes it does not jell in the manner you wish."

Tom rejoined the others by the fireside. Mama Harada placed another log in the fire. Her second daughter, Jean, came hurrying in with hot coffee and doughnuts.

"Come on, Tom," cried Minoru Harada, slapping his friend on the back. "Shake off the blues. This is our holiday. You know, the gardeners' vacation."

The two old men laughed and nodded their heads approvingly. "That's it, boy," agreed Tom's father. "It's the part of the game. Take it as they come. Sure enough, three straight weeks of rain is too much, but it will stop. Some day the sun will come out and you will have enough work."

Jean poured a cup of coffee for Tom. "They're right, Tom. Cheer up and make yourself comfortable. My boyfriend mustn't be a sourpuss."

Tom did not smile. He accepted the cup and placed it on the coffee table. His eyes turned in the direction of the window. "It isn't just the rain. It's something more, Jean. I'm worried about your garden and my garden and every other garden. Their fate is going to affect our lives."

"What do you mean, Tom? The gardens will take care of itself," laughed Papa Harada. "Rain, sun, wind… they cannot kill it. How will it be ruined?"

The old folks and the young turned curiously on the young man. Georgie, the thirteen-year-old boy who likes Gene Autry pictures, dimmed his favorite radio program. "War," Tom said quietly. "By war."

The room became silent. Mama Harada's face turned a trifle sallow, as she thought of her oldest son in the United States Army. Jean looked at her mother with concern. Finally, with gusto, Tom's father broke the silence.

"There will be no war in the Pacific. Never in our lifetime. My boy's crazy. He's too much of a pessimist," he declared.

"Tom, do you think there will be a war between the United States and Japan?" Mama Harada asked anxiously.

Tom looked at his father and then Papa Harada. "I don't know," he said.

"I pray for peace," Minoru cried fervently. "Give me thirty years of peace and I'll get on in the world. We Nisei are the luckiest guys in the world, to be born and raised in the United States. We got a fighting chance here. Better stake and opportunity here than anywhere else in the world."

Little Georgie laughed. "He's going to be a great singer."

"All right, Georgie. You keep still," ordered Minoru. He eagerly turned to Tom. "I'm going to try my hardest and become a singer. My teacher says I got a good voice. I don't like gardening the way you do, so I'm quitting at the first chance. If I have a few years I'll develop into a good singer."

Mama Harada smiled. "Minoru wants to be a singer more than anything else."

"Better he should stick to the family tradition… gardening," Papa Harada said. "Better he should use his vocal cords on his hired help and make money right away."

Tom rose once more from his seat and approached the window. His father's eyes followed his movement with concern. Jean got up to join Tom at the window.

Tom's father sadly shook his head. "Why don't you two kids go to the movies?" he suggested. "Here, take this five dollars and spend it. Have a good time."

Tom shook his head. "You don't want to go, do you, Jean?" he asked. She shook her head.

"Forget about the war possibility. You make the room and all of us fearful of the future which it shouldn't be," Tom's father said. "Forget about everything and take things lightly for a while. We came here to forget and pass the time away in friendship and pleasure."

"I can't forget its danger and possibility," cried Tom. "It won't be just the gardens churned up. It'll mean our lives and our democratic way of living, which we won't miss until we are deprived of it."

"I want an hour or two of relaxation this afternoon… to forget awhile," his father said.

Tom returned to his seat, leaving Jean alone by the window. "Pop, are you taking this war possibility lightly?"

His father shook his head and his figure slumped in the chair. Papa Harada added another log to the fire without a comment. Minoru perked up brightly.

"Well, I guess I have the only cheerful topic," he said. "Let's talk about my singing career. It won't cost anything or harm anyone."

"Fine!" cried Tom's father. "That's the spirit."

Jean came over to Tom's side with a checkerboard table. "Please, Tom, for my sake and your dad's. We'll play checkers again and see who will win this time."

"I'll win again!" cried Little Georgie, bringing his chair up.

"All right, Jean," Tom agreed.

They drew lots, and Little Georgie and Minoru started the elimination game. Jean went around offering coffee and doughnuts. When Tom finished his second cup he got up in search of a match. Jean watched him moving over to the window and looking out.

"Is it still raining, Tom?" she asked.

Tom nodded. "Plenty," he said.

She crossed the room and joined him, and the eyes of the young and the old awaited their reaction while the room became still.

—1944

107

Slant-Eyed Americans

Slant-Eyed Americans

My mother was commenting on the fine California weather. It was Sunday noon, December 7. We were having our lunch, and I had the radio going. "Let's take the afternoon off and go to the city," I said to Mother.

"All right. We shall go," she said dreamily. "Ah, four months ago my boy left Hayward to join the Army, and a fine send-off he had. Our good friends—ah, I shall never forget the day of his departure."

"We'll visit some of our friends in Oakland and then take in a movie," I said. "Care to come along, Papa?"

Father shook his head. "No, I'll stay home and take it easy."

"That's his heaven," Mother commented. "To stay home, read the papers over and over, and smoke his Bull Durham."

I laughed. Suddenly the musical program was cut off as a special announcement came over the air: At 7:25 this morning a squadron of Japanese bombing planes attacked Pearl Harbor. The battle is still in progress.

"What's this? Listen to the announcement," I cried, going to the radio.

Abruptly the announcement stopped and the musicale continued.

"What is it?" Mother asked. "What has happened?"

"The radio reports that Japanese planes attacked Hawaii this morning," I said incredulously. "It couldn't be true."

"It must be a mistake. Couldn't it have been a part of a play?" asked Mother.

I dialed other stations. Several minutes later one of the stations confirmed the bulletin.

"It must be true," Father said quietly.

I said, "Japan has declared war on the United States and Great Britain."

The room became quiet but for the special bulletin coming in every now and then.

"It cannot be true, yet it must be so," Father said over and over.

"Can it be one of those programs scaring the people about invasion?" Mother asked me.

"No, I'm sure this is a news report," I replied.

Mother's last ray of hope paled and her eyes became dull. "Why did it have to happen? The common people in Japan don't want war, and we don't want war. Here the people are peace-loving. Why cannot the peoples of the earth live together peacefully?"

"Since Japan declared war on the United States it'll mean that you parents of American citizens have become enemy aliens," I said.

"Enemy aliens," my mother whispered.

Night came but sleep did not come. We sat up late in the night hoping against hope that some good news would come, retracting the news of vicious attack and open hostilities.

"This is very bad for the people with Japanese faces," I said.

Father slowly shook his head.

"What shall we do?" asked Mother.

"What can we do?" Father said helplessly.

At the flower market next morning the growers were present but the buyers were scarce. The place looked empty and deserted. "Our business is shot to pieces," one of the boys said.

"Who'll buy flowers now?" another called.

Don Haley, the seedsman, came over looking bewildered. "I suppose you don't need seeds now."

We shook our heads.

"It looks bad," I said. "Will it affect your business?"

"Flower seed sale will drop but the vegetable seeds will move quicker," Don said. "I think I'll have to put more time on the vegetable seeds."

Nobu Hiramatsu, who had been thinking of building another greenhouse, joined us. He had plans to grow more carnations and expand his business.

"What's going to happen to your plans, Nobu?" asked one of the boys.

"Nothing. I'm going to sit tight and see how things turn out," he said.

"Flowers and war don't go together," Don said. "You cannot concentrate too much on beauty when destruction is going on about you."

"Sure, pretty soon we'll raise vegetables instead of flowers," Grasselli said.

A moment later the market opened and we went back to the tables to sell our flowers. Several buyers came in and purchased a little. The flowers didn't move at all. Just as I was about to leave the place I met Tom Yamashita, the Nisei gardener with a future.

"What are you doing here, Tom? What's the matter with your work?" I asked as I noticed his pale face.

"I was too sick with yesterday's news, so I didn't work," he said. "This is the end. I am done for."

"No, you're not. Buck up, Tom," I cried. "You have a good future, don't lose hope."

"Sometimes I feel all right. You are an American, I tell myself. Devote your energy and life to the American way of life. Long before this my mind was made up to become a true American. This morning my Caucasian American friends sympathized with me. I felt good and was grateful. Our opportunity has come to express ourselves and act. We are Americans in thought and action. I felt like leaping to work. Then I got sick again because I got to thinking that Japan was the country that attacked the United States. I wanted to bury myself for shame."

I put my hand on his shoulder. "We all feel the same way, Tom. We're human so we flounder around awhile when an unexpected and big problem confronts us, but now that situation has to be passed by. We can't live in the same stage long. We have to move along, face the reality no matter what's in store for us."

Tom stood silently.

"Let's go to my house and take the afternoon off," I suggested. "We'll face a new world tomorrow morning with boldness and strength. What do you say, Tom?"

"All right," Tom agreed.

At home Mother was anxiously waiting for me. When she saw Tom with me her eyes brightened. Tom Yamashita was a favorite of my mother's.

"Look, a telegram from Kazuo!" she cried to me, holding up an enve-lope. "Read it and tell me what he says."

I tore it open and read. "He wants us to send $45 for train fare. He has a good chance for a furlough."

Mother fairly leaped in the air with the news. She had not seen my brother for four months. "How wonderful! This can happen only in America."

Suddenly she noticed Tom looking glum, and pushed him in the house. "Cheer up, Tom. This is no time for young folks to despair. Roll up your sleeves and get to work. America needs you."

Tom smiled for the first time and looked at me.

"See, Tom?" I said. "She's quick to recover. Yesterday she was wilted, and she's seventy-three."

"Tom, did you go to your gardens today?" she asked him.

"No."

"Why not?" she asked, and then added quickly. "You young men should work hard all the more, keeping up the normal routine of life. You ought to know, Tom, that if everybody dropped their work everything would go to seed. Who's going to take care of the gardens if you won't?"

Tom kept still.

Mother poured tea and brought the cookies. "Don't worry about your old folks. We have stayed here to belong to the American way of life. Time will tell our true purpose. We remained in America for perma-nence—not for temporary convenience. We common people need not fear."

"I guess you are right," Tom agreed.

"And America is right. She cannot fail. Her principles will stand the test of time and tyranny. Someday aggression will be outlawed by all nations."

Mother left the room to prepare the dinner. Tom got up and began to walk up and down the room. Several times he looked out the window and watched the wind blow over the field.

"Yes, if the gardens are ruined I'll rebuild them," he said. "I'll take charge of every garden in the city. All the gardens of America for that matter. I'll rebuild them as fast as the enemies wreck them. We'll have nature on our side and you cannot crush nature."

I smiled and nodded. "Good for you! Tomorrow we'll get up early in the morning and work, sweat, and create. Let's shake on it."

We solemnly shook hands, and by the grip of his fingers I knew he was ready to lay down his life for America and for his gardens.

"No word from him yet," Mother said worriedly. "He should have arrived yesterday. What's happened to him?"

It was eight in the evening, and we had had no word from my brother for several days. "He's not coming home tonight. It's too late now," I said. "He should have arrived in Oakland this morning at the latest."

Our work had piled up and we had to work late into the night. There were still some pompons to bunch. Faintly the phone rang in the house.

"The phone!" cried Mother excitedly. "It's Kazuo, sure enough."

In the flurry of several minutes I answered the phone, greeted my brother, and was on my way to San Leandro to drive him home. On the way I tried to think of the many things I wanted to say. From the moment I spotted him waiting on the corner I could not say the thing I wanted to. I took his bag and he got in the car, and for some time we did not say anything. Then I asked him how the weather had been in Texas and how he had been.

"We were waiting for you since yesterday," I said. "Mother is home getting the supper ready. You haven't eaten yet, have you?"

He shook his head. "The train was late getting into Los Angeles. We were eight hours behind time and I should have reached San Francisco this morning around eight."

Reaching home it was the same way. Mother could not say anything. "We have nothing special tonight, wish we had something good."

"Anything would do, Mama," my brother said.

Father sat in the room reading the papers but his eyes were over the sheet and his hands were trembling. Mother scurried about getting his supper ready. I sat across the table from my brother, and in the silence which was action I watched the wave of emotions in the room. My brother was aware of it too. He sat there without a word, but I knew he understood. Not many years ago he was the baby of the family, having never been away from home. Now he was on his own, his quiet confidence actually making him appear larger. Keep up the fire, that was his

115

company's motto. It was evident that he was a soldier. He had gone beyond life-and-death matter, where the true soldiers of war or peace must travel, and had returned.

For five short days we went about our daily task, picking and bunching the flowers for Christmas, eating heavy meals, and visiting the intimates. It was as if we were waiting for the hour of his departure, the time being so short. Every minute was crowded with privacy, friends, and nursery work. Too soon the time for his train came, but the family had little to say.

"Kazuo, don't worry about home or me," Mother said as we rode into town.

"Take care of yourself," my brother told her.

At the 16th Street station, Mother's close friend was waiting for us. She came to bid my brother goodbye. We had fifteen minutes to wait. My brother bought a copy of The Coast to see if his cartoons were in.

"Are you in this month's issue?" I asked.

"I haven't seen it yet," he said, leafing the pages. "Yes, I'm in. Here it is."

"Good!" I said. "Keep trying hard. Someday peace will come, and when you return laughter will reign once again."

My mother showed his cartoon to her friend. The train came in and we got up. It was a long one. We rushed to the Los Angeles-bound coach.

Mother's friend shook hands with my brother. "Give your best to America. Our people's honor depends on you Nisei soldiers."

My brother nodded and then glanced at Mother. For a moment her eyes twinkled and she nodded. He waved goodbye from the platform. Once inside the train we lost him. When the train began to move my mother cried, "Why doesn't he pull up the shades and look out? Others are doing it."

We stood and watched until the last of the train was lost in the night of darkness.

—1949

The Travelers

The Travelers

At the gatehouse in front of the administration building stood the travelers, waiting for their names to be checked off the passenger list. Along the fence were lined their friends and well-wishers. The day was fine for a last farewell at the gate, as the crowd of several hundred persons would assure. Here and there the Internal Security workers darted as last-minute communications occupied their attention. A truck bearing the baggage of relocatees slowly cut a path into the crowd and stopped beyond the fence. The travelers' eyes anxiously peered into the canvas-covered truck for a reassuring glance at their belongings. The load was a good one for there were nine persons, including a child, heading for all points east.

At last the overdue bus for the town of Delta appeared on the scene. A flurry of cries and gestures sent off the nine as the group boarded the bus. Now the shoppers to Delta milled about the gate for the choice seats remaining in the car. Their grinning and nonchalant faces, as they walked beyond the gate to the car, bore the jibes of their acquaintances who reminded them not to get lost in town and to be sure and return to Topaz.

For a final check-up a clerk boarded the bus and counted the heads, and the driver, racing the motor, impatiently watched for the "go" signal. As the bus pulled away from the gatehouse, the passengers frantically looked back and waved to the people along the fence. The car picked up speed and the folks settled back in their seats. Now the hospital was passed; the water tank and the MP barracks became blurred and a speck in the distance.

A small child who was clinging to her mother's hand stood in her seat with her nose flat against the window. "Look, Mommy. Our camp looks like a toy house now," she cried.

The mother gazed over her shoulder and nodded her head. "Yes, Mary. In a few minutes we shall see no more of it. Topaz will become a memory."

The little girl began to sob as she settled down in her seat. "I'm going to miss Sachi and Dorothy and Miye… "

"Hush, child," soothed the Issei woman. "You shall make many new friends. Do not cry."

After a while the child dried her tears and blew her nose with a handkerchief, and presently her eyes followed the horizon, sweeping at a glance the autumn scene in the foreground. The corn stalks were turning brown; the harvested alfalfa fields looked bare and dry and the trees had shed their leaves.

Behind the little girl sat an aged woman who now leaned forward and patted the head of the child. "You're a very brave little girl," she said, smiling. As the child's mother glanced back, she addressed her, "Where are you heading for? You are courageous—an Issei very seldom relocates by herself."

The younger woman smiled and patted her girl's shoulder. "I am not alone—she's with me. We are going to Kansas City for her education. There I shall enter the domestic world again, and Mary shall go to school. I want so badly to give her the best education that I am willing to slave and scrimp the rest of my days."

The aged woman looked dubious but nodded sympathetically. She looked about the car with interest. She could easily tell apart the relocatees from the shoppers by the respective type of clothes they wore. Her ears caught the conversation of the shoppers' group.

"My husband wants me to get a pair of small hinges and a gallon of ivory paint. Also he told me to look around for electric sockets and plugs."

"Do you know what I'm going to do first? Buy clothes and groceries? No! I'm going to get me a couple of hamburgers and coffee at the restaurant, and then at Thornton's gorge myself on a chocolate nut sundae. That's what I'll do."

"I have a lot of birthday presents to buy for my children. Yes, three of the kids will be having their birthdays in the next four months. Have you been out to town lately? What have they in the way of children's toys and clothes?"

The aged woman studied the travelers with growing curiosity. There was a young girl in a smart Chesterfield coat reading the train schedule, and across from her sat another Nisei girl, her face flushed and her eyes sparkling with adventure. Surely, a pair of relocatees, thought the old woman.

The bus began to slow down, and the eyes of the passengers looked ahead. In front of the MP gatehouse the car stopped and a soldier came aboard to check the passenger list. He tallied the number of names on the paper with the number of heads and jumped off, waving the bus away.

Once more the journey to Delta was resumed, and the folks settled back in their seats. The aged woman continued gazing at her fellow travelers. Once, twice, she smiled to herself. She noticed the solemnity and independence of the relocatees and the boisterousness and companionship of the shoppers' group. "On the way... our journey," she whispered softly to herself. "Travelers... we are all travelers on the earth."

In the middle of her thoughts, the woman sitting in front of her spoke to her. "May I ask where you are going? I don't suppose you are going shopping. You don't look it."

The old woman chuckled softly, and then grasping the sleeve of the young man sitting beside her said, "This is my boy and I am seeing him off. Roy is on his way to Camp Shelby."

For the first time the mother and her child noticed the youth in a private's uniform. Mary's eyes were quick to see that the soldier was a recent volunteer. His shoulder insignia was missing. The little girl became shy as the soldier's humor-filled eyes met hers.

Now the coach crossed the overpass and reached the downhill grade. The soldier's eyes followed the course of the Sevier River until the steep bank masked the scene.

"In a few minutes we'll be in Delta," a voice informed the crowd in general.

At last, thought the soldier. His eyes anxiously looked ahead but presently he turned his gaze on his mother. Their eyes met. "Don't worry about me, Mama. I'll be all right," he said.

The mother slowly nodded her head.

As the bus turned left at the crossroad, the eyes of the passengers were focused to the right on a big bird that floated indifferently in the air.

"How symmetrical and natural!" exclaimed someone in the group.

"Picture of an idyl," cried another. "How lucky the birds are. They can live in spite of a war-torn world."

"The people, too, will survive this war," quickly commented the soldier's mother from the rear.

In an instant the attention of the travelers was on the tiny old woman sitting beside the soldier. The girl whose sparkling eyes spoke adventure gazed respectfully at her, and smiling thus, her features effused silent applause. In a fraction of a second the soldier caught the lively eyes of the girl. A moment later their eyes met again. The town of Delta loomed ahead.

Beautiful, thought the soldier. What have I been doing all this time in Topaz? Who is she? Where is she going? Instinctively, he looked at his watch. Time was short. He gathered up his heavy army coat and duffle bag. The bus turned left into the dirt road that wound up at the station. In front of the baggage room the bus stopped to let off the train passengers and the soldier's mother.

The soldier and his mother stood in front of the station, watching the others enter the station to purchase their tickets. Soon a party of Caucasian travelers and their friends appeared from the waiting room. Among them were a sailor and a corporal, presumably returning to their duty.

"Let's go inside and see if the train is on time," suggested the boy to his mother.

Inside, the small waiting room was packed with Salt Lake-bound travelers. Roy and his mother stood near the center of the room, where the unfired coal stove was located.

"The train is on time, Mama," he announced to her, looking at the bulletin board. "It's pulling in at 2:30."

The mother nodded her head. "Only thirty minutes more, Roy," she said.

A youth of eighteen or nineteen years of age approached the old woman, "There's a seat for you, oba-san. Take it because you'll have some time to wait yet."

The mother politely refused the first time but with repeated offerings, she thanked the Nisei and accepted the seat on the bench.

"Where are you going... to college?" asked the soldier to the hatless youth who offered the seat.

The latter agreed. "I'm going to the University of Wisconsin. That's in Madison, Wisconsin, you know."

"So you're going to Wisconsin, eh?" questioned a dapper Nisei in a well-tailored suit and topcoat. "Boy, we Nisei are certainly traveling nowadays. We're like the seeds in the wind. Now, I'm going to New York. I always wanted to see the big city but I was a tied-down man. Here I am now with an opportunity to start all over again."

"You look successful," commented the soldier. "What were you doing before the war?"

"I used to operate a drive-in market in the south... Los Angeles, I mean," replied the man. "I used to have a good business but had to sell the place for almost nothing. Oh well, that's past."

The soldier was curious. He asked the man what his purpose was in going to New York, but his eyes searched for the girl he saw in the bus. She was seated at the end of the bench talking with the girl who still held the train schedule in her gloved hand.

The dapper Nisei shrugged his shoulders. "I'm just going to New York on a hunch. I want to feel my way around before I settle down. By the time I call my wife and kids I want to be sitting pretty."

"You aren't thinking of going back to California?" asked the young student.

"No," he said emphatically. "To my way of thinking, California is a poor proposition for Nisei. Why should I wait several more years for an admission permit or stall around for the postwar period before staking myself in the outside world?"

A tall Nisei with powerful shoulders who was leaning against the wall and talking to a baggage man chucked his cigarette away and approached the group. "You folks travelin' too?" he said pleasantly. "Anyone goin' my way... Akron, Ohio?"

The dapper Nisei chuckled softly. "It seems we have different choices.

This fellow here is going to study in Madison, Wisconsin, and, of course, this soldier is going to Shelby, Mississippi. And I'm heading for New York. By the way, where is that Issei woman with the child going?"

"She's going to Missouri... Kansas City," said the soldier.

"And where you girls goin'?" asked the Nisei with hefty shoulders, turning to the two Nisei girls.

The soldier watched the girl with the sparkling eyes glance at the group before replying.

"I am going to Chicago... a job is waiting for me in the office of a big firm, and she," indicating her companion, "is getting married in Philadelphia."

Fascinating, thought the soldier. I'd like to know her better. Oh, why does life offer me things at the last moment?

The Nisei with the powerful shoulders shifted his weight from one foot to the other, grinning at the girls. "Chicago... Philadelphia... Kansas City... New York... Camp Shelby... Madison... Akron. Ain't it strange we meet here? One hour and we part once and for all. Maybe we'll never meet again, eh?"

"I'm going out to see if the train is in sight," the student announced, going to the door.

The girl who was bound for a Chicago office giggled excitedly and her voice trembled a little. "This is my first trip away from the folks. Oh, I'm so thrilled. Ever since graduating from high school I've been a domestic worker, and now I am going to be a stenographer... a white-collar job. Isn't it exciting?"

"I'm a farmer from Northern California," said the Nisei with the big shoulders. "My friend calls me from Ohio. He says there's plenty of farms... many hundred-acre farms for sale at reasonable prices. Can you imagine? For two to four thousand dollars you can buy such farms with farmhouses and buildings. Yeah, even a lot costs two thousand back in California."

The soldier's mother beckoned her son, and the latter walked over to the bench. "Isn't it about time for the train to arrive, Roy?" she asked anxiously.

"It ought to be here in five minutes, Mama," said her son. He helped his mother to her feet.

"Let us wait outside," the mother said.

The Chicago-bound girl smiled at him, and he hesitated in his steps. For a second his mind raced with frenzied thoughts: Hello, lovely. Let's get acquainted; let's travel through life together for a while. Okay?

Then suddenly, resolutely, the soldier lifted his head high and turned on his heels, heading for the door. The young student ran in excitedly, "The train... it's coming, folks."

Outside, the group watched the distant speck on the horizon growing ever larger. Soon the virgin Utah sky of the moment was darkened with black smoke. The Challenger had reached Delta on time.

The little group rushed forward, their companionship of a moment ago forgotten, and they sought seats in several cars. Only the soldier and his mother stalled for time. "Don't worry about me, Mama. I'll be all right, so take good care of yourself," he said.

The mother waved her hand as the train slowly began to move.

Once on the train the clan dispersed. Soldiers, bright and friendly, were everywhere. And the Japanese faces were now lost in the crowd as they should be.

As the soldier's mother slowly trudged along the dirt road toward Delta, a car stopped alongside her. A Caucasian and his wife were signaling her to get into the car. From the rear of the sedan a girl opened the door for her. For a moment, she hesitated and then said, "Thank you."

"Come in. We'll give you a ride to town," the girl said, smiling.

The aged woman climbed aboard with the help of the girl. All the way to town, which was only a few blocks away from the station, the group did not chat, for they had no common language, but understood the trials and errors of a traveler's way.

— 1943

Letters

TOSHIO MORI was twenty-eight years old and still working up to twelve hours daily at the family's nursery when his first story was published in *Coast* magazine. The published work, "The Brothers," came to the attention of established California writer William Saroyan, who got in touch with Mori through the *Coast* editors and began encouraging him to get more of his work into print. By the early forties, Mori's stories had made an impression upon the American literary scene, appearing in magazines such as *The Clipper, Iconograph, Writer's Forum* and *Common Ground*.

With enough material for an entire short-story manuscript and with the support of varied literary sources, Mori began searching for a publisher. The following letters are from Mori's correspondence with Saroyan from 1942 to 1950. Saroyan proved to be a tireless and valuable supporter, writing letters of introduction on Mori's behalf to all of the major American publishing houses. While the book was considered by other publishers, *Yokohama, California* by Toshio Mori was finally announced with a Spring 1942 release date by James H. Gipson, publisher of Caxton Printers in Idaho.

What remains remarkable about these letters is not only *Yokohama California*'s early publication history and the strength of Saroyan's support of Mori's work, but the faith Mori sustained in his writing and the imminent publication of his first book, even in the face of the mass evacuation of Japanese Americans that would force Mori out of California. In fact, it should be noted that Mori continues his literary camaraderie with Saroyan from an internment camp in Utah. Caxton Printers would postpone the publication of *Yokohama, California* until 1949 and Mori would continue to write despite the hardships faced during the war. However, the impact that the evacuation and internment experience had on Japanese Americans such as Mori, financially draining an entire community and thus curtailing blossoming artistic careers, is immeasurable.

1470-164th ave.
San Leandro, Calif.
February 8, 1942.

Dear Bill:

I just received a letter from the Caxton informing that Mr. Gipson is making a trip to San Francisco to see you and me. He is at present in the East on business and expects to be in San Francisco about February 24–26. His temporary quarters will be at St. Francis Hotel. I know you are busy so I hate to put you to a lot of trouble but I'm asking you whether you'll be able to meet us. Mr. Gipson would very much like to meet you and settle things about the book.

If you should be in Hollywood at the time and unable to be in San Francisco I will tell him to get in touch with you there. However, he would like to see us together if it's possible. I believe he wishes to discuss with you on several points, including the publishing date. If we can get together it'd be swell but that depends on your working schedule. If you'll tell me when you'll be free, if it's possible, I'd like to inform Mr. Gipson ahead of time.

I am working on the stories you suggested and hope to have it finished soon.

With many thanks for your help and the warmest regards to you and your family,

Yours sincerely,
Toshio Mori

1470-164th ave.
San Leandro, Calif.
March 1, 1942.

Dear Bill:

I want to thank you again and again for taking your valuable time to help me with my first book. I'm sure that in such a situation as I am in you are the only one who would help. I am very grateful. Mr. Gipson came away with a lasting impression of you. He asked me especially to extend his best wishes and thanks to you.

Last Friday he invited me to a breakfast at his hotel and I had several hours of talk. First thing he told me was his meeting with you. He certainly was grateful for your reception, and he was much overcome by your personality and greatness.

I think you are familiar with his purpose so I won't say much about it. As you may know, he personally thinks the title "Yokohama, California" is all right. He told me to think it over, saying the stories would right any misconception of the title. I don't know. So far, I have been thinking of possible title with no success. I'm going to leave it up to you and Mr. Gipson. Meanwhile, I'll try and find another good one.

I am sorry those two stories did not reach you in time. Mr. Gipson told me some of your generous aids, and I appreciate it very much.

With warmest regards, and much thanks,

Yours sincerely,
Toshio Mori

1470-164th ave.
San Leandro, Calif.
March 24, 1942.

Dear Bill:

I have just received a letter from Mr. Gipson of the Caxton Printers on the publication matter. A tentative publication date of November 15, 1942 has been set for *Yokohama, California*. Although the date is later than the one you suggested I guess it is for the best. I thank you for your sincere aid. Mr. Gipson was telling me that you wished an early issue of the book, but he said he must confer with his associates on the matter. He promised the earliest possible date.

As you probably know the Japanese must evacuate from the West Coast. We are expecting the evacuation order any minute. My destination is unknown at present. We may end in the government camp. I shall inform you from time to time. In a way this new experience may benefit me although it may be trying. I hope to be with the people.

I hope to write you before I leave the present address. If I should find it impossible then I will write you at the first chance from the new address.

With best of luck to your new work, *Human Comedy!* Once again thanks for all the work you have done for me and for my coming book.

With warm regards and best of health to you,

> Cordially yours,
> Toshio

29-11-D,
Topaz, Utah.
September 16, 1943.
Thursday, 7:30 P.M.

Dear Bill:

How are you? I hope everything is all right with you and the family. It has been a long time since I last wrote you, which was back in Spring, 1942, while I was still in Tanforan. Of course, I have been keeping up with your progress through the papers, magazines, radio programs, the movies. And congratulations upon your marriage to a beautiful young lady! And the best of luck to you as a soldier of the U.S. Army! I must apologize to you for delaying this belated letter.

Perhaps you have been wondering what had happened to little Toshio Mori who used to visit you in San Francisco in the peacetime era. After the Tanforan episode, I joined the trek of our people to the Central Utah Relocation Project which is around 145 miles southwest of Salt Lake City. It is situated in the Sevier Desert, the second largest desert area in Utah, and our constant discomforts are the nature's undoings.

We have too much of dust and wind and too little of rain, green living things and adequate opportunities for the folks. Personally, I have enough material to keep me busy for a long time to come, but for the average people this center life does not inspire initiative. And when such conditions fall upon the usually hardworking Japanese, there is bound to be frustration and defeatism. Some people keep up their spirit through an outlet of anger, but the great majority of the folks comply to the situation as inevitable as all good people do all over the world.

Back in Tanforan you suggested that I ought to write a short novel about Tanforan Center life, but I wasn't ready then. In Tanforan I took things easy for a while, just observing and experiencing things that were so new to me. I came to Topaz back in October, 1942, with 8000 odd members of the Bay Region district. Ever since the induction days, I have been a historian for this relocation center, documenting major and minor events. The work is made for me, and I have profited considerably. I head the historical documentation section, and our staff manage to find fun in our work, which is something in a center. But I have another news for you which I know you would be glad to know about.

On February 12th of this year I got to work on my first novel. On August 22nd I finished *Send These, the Homeless*. It consists of 32 chapters, and at present totals 471 pages. About halfway through I contacted Frank Morley and he wrote that he was anxious to see the novel, so I submitted it to Harcourt. Last month I received their house's decision and it is enclosed. It was rejected, but I still believe in its value. I submitted in the first draft form, and I can readily see some of the weak spots. I am rewriting and editing the whole thing. I think you can guess the theme of the novel. The story begins on December 7th, 1941, and ends somewhere in March, 1943. It is a part of the many novels I hope to write about, if time and circumstance permit. I have several other publishers interested in the first novel, among them John Farrar of Farrar and Rinehart, Quincy Howe of Simon and Schuster. So far I have been on my own, submitting the mss. directly to the publisher, but with the latest experience with the express service I find that I lose much valuable time when timeliness counts a lot in the case of a Japanese American novel. Don't you think such a novel draws interest of the Americans at this moment? There is one agent I know, A. L. Fierst, who says the topic is red hot and wishes to handle the book for me. I would like to have your opinion before I do anything this time.

I have another novel in the making, *Tomorrow Is Coming, Children*. It will be considerably shorter than the first one. Although that book of short stories to be published by the Caxtons has been held up for the duration by the publisher, I have found much material in the Japanese problem since then.

Your great book and motion picture, *Human Comedy*, has captivated the Nisei. Our Topaz Public Library has a copy of your latest work, and it is most popular and always reserved weeks ahead. My brother who is now stationed at Camp Shelby, Miss. sent me a copy of *Human Comedy*, and since reading it once on the arrival I haven't seen the book. It is being passed around the center so much that now I don't know who has it. My brother has seen the picture at three cities, Salt Lake, Chicago, and Detroit, and at each picture house he noticed the audience weeping and sighing. And when the common people can be thus moved, it must be the greatest of the greats. I wish someday I have the opportunity of seeing the film version of the *Human Comedy*.

According to my brother, a soldier has very little time for himself so I feel that you are pressed for time. I'll close now and write again. Please take good care of yourself. I hope all this turmoil and tribulations will contribute, in the end, to the good. It just happens that we were born to live out our lives according to the fate of time. I hope to welcome the day when I shall once more meet you.

With warmest regards,

> Yours,
> Toshio

1470-164th ave.
San Leandro, Calif.,
February 10, 1950

Dear Bill,

First of all, I wish to thank you for writing those introductions to your recent books, *Don't Go Away Mad* and *The Assyrian*. They made me feel glad for everything, and they make life worthwhile. I hope every serious writer reads them.

Since I just received my copies of the two books, I read the play *Don't Go Away Mad*, which is a rare work of art. I have read it three times. The more I read the more I received. I think you gave lots in writing and living it. I got a wonderful experience from it. There is growth and richness. I wish there were more like you writing in this world. It would be better all around. As far as I'm concerned, you're the only living writer I truly respect. This isn't because you've encouraged me in writing but I believe you are the beacon of light. You are far ahead of the pack. I always have a feeling that you will be more fully understood of what you have and are doing many, many years from now. Maybe I feel this way because I want to go my way just as you are going your way. Anyhow I feel humble and happy that you are leading the way by giving more than anyone else.

Through your suggestion, I got to know Yasuo Kuniyoshi when he came to teach at Mills College last summer. He is great and also a wonderful person. Last month he sent me his drawing which has become my favorite.

Thanks very much, Bill, for telling editors of my work. Jack Goodman of Simon and Schuster wrote me, asking to see my novel. He saw it but the final decision was against acceptance. This book is my recently completed *Woman From Hiroshima*. John Fisher of *Harper's* and John Hall Wheelock of *Scribner's* have seen it too and all of them liked it but no offers. I have just heard from George Cronyn who has the manuscript, and he tells he has submitted it to your editor and friend, Robert Giroux of Harcourt. I told Cronyn that you mentioned Giroux for my next book sometime ago. Anyhow I want to thank you for going out of your way to put in a good word for me to Giroux. I am a lucky one.

When you do come out to San Francisco again, I would like to have you over for dinner or go out for a sukiyaki in S.F.

My very best wishes to you,

Sincerely,
Toshio

The Brothers Murata

a novel

To my brother Kazuo,
ex-sergeant, 442nd Infantry,
to my parents
and my family

1

The crowd surged forward as the train for points south pulled into the station. Soldiers and sailors dominated the scene. Out of the civilian contingent a small group of five youths emerged.

They each carried a grip. They were friends for they pushed and joshed each other unmercifully. As they noticed a trio of pretty women, they whistled softly and made way for them. They grinned spontaneously. "You future GI wolves!" muttered one to the rest.

The boys chuckled, and they jostled one another good-naturedly. They were a typical bunch of young fellows in America—full of wisecracks and capable of boyish mischief. They were representative Americans but for their Oriental facial features—they were Nisei from Topaz.

The five boys scrambled through the cars for vacant seats. They found five vacant chairs in the men's rest room. They sweated profusely.

"How do you feel, Hiro?" asked a tall youth, offering his cigarette to the group.

Hiro Murata smiled lazily. "Never felt better in my life, Yosh. The trip's been good for me."

"Fort Douglas didn't get you down?" Yosh Yoshida asked. "How'd you like the army routine?"

Hiro grinned at his chum. "A little different from our camp life, eh? Well, I'm going to take hard knocks and make myself like it."

"What about you, Yosh?" asked a chunky boy named Tad Aihara. "How do you feel as a 1A?"

"How do you feel, Tad? And how do all of you feel? You all passed," Yosh said.

"Okay, Okay," Tad said, grinning and glancing at the group.

Servicemen came in and out of the room. They stood at the wash basin for a snatch of smoke. They did not raise their eyes at the sight of five Nisei. They asked for time, for matches, for information. They went out after a spell and then another group of soldiers came into the room.

"Pretty soon we'll be like them," commented Hiro. "We'll have a chance to show what we're made of."

"Such an honor," Yosh cracked slyly.

"This is what we've been waiting for, you dope," said Tad.

Tack Saiki slumped lazily in his seat. "I wish to Christ I were home— good old Topaz. I'm sick of the city lights already. Me for home."

"Tack's a mama's good little boy," Tad said. He looked at the one in the corner reading a comic book. "Susumu, what's eating you? Why so quiet?"

"Nothing," replied Susumu.

"Anything to say? Are you sick?"

"No, I'm okay. I've got no kick coming." Susumu went back to his comics.

The train rolled southward from Salt Lake City. Snow remained on the distant high peaks. Once or twice snowflakes pelted the train windows. The little group in the rest room gazed out boredly.

"I bet it's hot as hell in Topaz," Hiro said skeptically.

"Home will mean more to us after this," Tack said, yawning. "We'll begin to miss camp life—some of us."

"What do you mean—some of us?" asked Tad curiously.

Tack looked meaningfully at the group but they missed the point. "You know what's brewing at the camp."

"No."

"Hell you don't."

"Honest, Tack. Put me wise," Tad said. "I don't think the rest know either."

"I bet Yosh knows about it," Tack said. "Don't you, Yosh?"

"If you're talking about some boys bucking the draft, I do."

"There it is, Tad. I suppose that was a secret to you."

"First time I heard about it," Tad said. He turned to Hiro. "Did you hear about boys evading the draft in Topaz?"

Hiro shook his head. "I can't see why a Nisei should refuse to fight for his country—unless he's a coward."

Tack gravely looked at his friend. "Hiro, do you know that your brother is one of them?"

For a moment Hiro did not comprehend. "Who are you talking about? Frank? You must be mistaken, Tack," he said slowly and quietly.

"No, Hiro," Tack said. "I know for sure it's Frank Murata—your older brother."

The group watched Hiro silently. "There are several Frank Muratas in camp," Hiro said.

"I know," said Tack quietly. "Ask Yosh—your sidekick. He won't lie. Ask him."

Hiro turned to his best friend. The latter hesitated and then nodded his head. "I won't believe it till Frank says so. It can't be my brother—not Frank."

He glanced about the group for affirmation. The boys sat silently—without comments. He went to the fountain and drank deliberately. As he straightened he saw his reflection in the mirror and noticed the pallor of his face.

2

He walked toward the well-lit dining hall, noticing the stream of people entering the building. The overhanging clouds threatened with rain, and a sharp wind chilled his skin. What a night to be out, he thought, as he passed the cozy-looking barracks. Yosh must be waiting for me.

He felt better as he came under the dining hall lights. Yosh came forward eagerly, taking his arm. "You're late, Hiro. The hall's packed but I've got two seats saved," he said.

They took their seats in the middle row. Every bench space was taken and the latecomers stood along the walls waiting for the chairman to open the session. Hiro's eyes looked about eagerly.

"Encouraging, isn't it?" he asked Yosh. "What a turnout. Topaz is showing its true form."

"Must be five hundred here tonight. Almost enough for a battalion," Yosh said.

Hiro smiled happily. Frank must be here, he thought. He must be here, for he left home early. His eyes searched about the hall but could not locate him. Then Yosh, as if on the same thought, leaned forward and pointed out Frank.

"See? Over there in the fifth row—he's with his friends."

Hiro chuckled, his eyes shining full. "Yes, he's here." He's here, he thought. He's here for this patriotic rally. Tack's wrong; Yosh's wrong. Frank is okay. He's all right. Frank might be noncommittal but his heart was true. He could overlook Frank's frequent absence at home. Now he could relax, sit back and watch the proceedings without worry.

The meeting progressed as he expected. Strong leaders rallied the

audience with tact, and voices of testament came from the ranks of volunteers. He felt warm and sleepy, so smoothly the proceedings advanced.

He listened to the statements of the bona fide army volunteers. There
was Tad Aihara's chunky form standing astride on the stage and facing
the audience. Tad made a simple speech—the kind of talk he would
have made. He volunteered, Tad voiced, because he felt it was his duty.
He wanted to drive his stake into the soil of his country. He was thinking of tomorrow—not solely of today. Yes, Tad talked straight. He was
straight. But Tad was Tad. How about others—boys who had not quite
made up their minds and those who merely came to hear? Why was the
hall so quiet?

Then out of the dimension of his complacency Hiro awoke with a
jerk. Almost everyone appeared to be out of order. The chairman rapped
his gavel ceaselessly without results. Scores were standing, demanding
the floor and shaking their fists. Then others joined in, clamoring for
silence. Yosh cupped his hand and shouted in Hiro's ear, but he could
not hear. Finally Yosh gave up.

Who are here? Hiro, thought, his suspicions aroused. Who have come?
Order, order. We must have order.

Order was not completely restored again. Raised fists and threats
clouded the hall. No speaker held the floor for long. Small groups, planted
in every section of the room, shouted down the once-powerful leaders
among the volunteers. Who were these oppositionists? He could smash
them if he were only certain who they were. He would crack them down.

Yosh clutched his arm as he pointed to a solidly built man who stood
impressively in front of the stage. He raised his hand for order, and gradually the noise subsided.

"Who is he?" Hiro asked his chum, impressed by his influence. "Do
you know him?"

"He's John Tabe—the leader of the opposition," Yosh replied.

John Tabe, John Tabe, thought Hiro. He must remember that name.
His eyes narrowed as he sized up the man. A troublemaker. Hiro was
about to call it to Yosh's attention when he noticed his friend's rapt
attention to John Tabe's talk. He decided not to tell Yosh.

John Tabe was demanding that a concerted action should be taken
on the restoration of civil rights for Nisei before such talk as reinstitution

of selective service ever be mentioned. Another youth immediately stood up dramatically:

"Remember, you Nisei! Don't forget the injustice of evacuation! Demand first or you won't get anything. Remember how we meekly obeyed the evacuation order? Now, look where we are!"

In his mind, Hiro coined a new word for himself. Disloyalists—the goddamn disloyalists. They aren't fighting for civil rights; they're thinking of themselves! His lips pressed tightly. His laugh was bitter. They're not interested in civil rights—they're bucking the draft. Nothing but a lousy welter of speeches.

Suddenly Hiro's head snapped back. He looked across the stage and then back at the latest speaker. His eyes opened wider. In that second he thought of his dead father and his parting words. "Stay in America. Be a good American—always. Live, grow, and die American."

He slumped in his seat, his face down and buried.

"Frank Murata," whispered Yosh almost to himself. "He's upholding John Tabe."

His head ringing bells, Hiro did not hear his friend. He could not tear his thoughts away from his father's wish. Why, Frank? Why the change of heart? Have you forgotten Papa? Come back, Frank. Come back.

Now the evening's progress did not matter. He ventured to gaze at the spot where Frank had stood, and there he was sitting in the middle of a circle—alive, aggressive and cool-headed. He must get in touch with him—tonight, now. He must show the way; he must convince Frank. How? His brother was intelligent, a far better thinker than he. Frank was practical and a rationalist. And he was emotional and impulsive. What are his arguments for volunteering? Were there more to reveal or express than Tad Aihara had done a few minutes ago? Could he handle Frank? He must handle him.

The clouds still unbroken, the night was gloomy and black. Hiro was immediately in the dark after he left Yosh on the roadway. About him the scattering people scurried homeward. He did not attempt to hail his block friends. He wanted to be alone. Yet he looked backward to see if Frank were coming down the road. Tonight he must get hold of him and talk to him.

Up ahead he saw half a dozen youths standing in the middle of the

road, smoking and talking little. Their dark figures were unrecogniz-
able. Hiro stepped off the road and attempted to pass them.

"Hiro, hold up a minute," a voice boomed at him.

He hesitated and then came forward. The voice belonged to John
Tabe. There were faces he did not know, and then he saw Frank. Frank,
Frank. Let's go home, he thought. But they did not leave him alone
for long.

"Hiro, we wanted to see you," John Tabe was saying. "And it might
just as well be now. Were you there at the meeting tonight?"

Hiro nodded his head looking at Frank all the while. "What do you
want of me?"

"We could use a guy like you. How about joining up? Frank's in already," John Tabe said.

Hiro remained silent. They watched with sharp beaks like hawks,
and they reveled in their strength of number. Better come in if you know
what's good for you, their attitude seemed to shout. Come across easily,
Hiro. Time's a-flying.

"Wha'dya say?" coaxed one stranger.

"Are you with us, Hiro?" John Tabe asked again.

"Don't rush him, boys," warned Frank, coming forward anxiously.
"Give him time. Let him decide for himself."

"For Christ's sake, how much time he wants?" cried a husky youth
impatiently.

"Hurry up, fellow. We're freezing out here," another voice said.

Hiro now studied each face. He hated every one of the faces till he
got to Frank's. They faced each other unflinchingly. "Count me out,
boys. I'm not interested," he said quietly.

The men stood hesitatingly. Their arrogance became stronger but they
faltered. John Tabe was cool when he spoke, "Don't say we didn't warn
you, Hiro. We'll leave you alone as long as you don't put your nose into
our business. Get it, Hiro?"

"And what is your business?" asked Hiro testily.

John Tabe casually lit a cigarette. "Anything that concerns tonight's
problem. Stay clear of that and you'll be okay."

The boys edged away restlessly. "Come on, John. Let's scram." Frank
joined them, leaving Hiro in the middle of the road.

"Frank, Frank," Hiro called. "I want to speak to you."

Frank did not stop. He looked back, gesturing with his hand. "I'll see you later."

He took several steps in their direction. "Frank, wait up. I want to see you now." He attempted to follow them but lost them in the dark.

3

They waited for Frank at the supper table. He looked at his watch. Frank was twenty minutes late. Mother had reheated the mess hall food several times on their electric stove. She pottered about the stove patiently. He drummed his fingers on the table. Frank is drifting away from the family, he thought.

"Frank must be busy at the office," Mama said for a way of excuse.

"Yes, he must be busy," replied Hiro, watching the slight figure of his mother working wholeheartedly for the comforts of her family. She looked peaked and tired ever since he had volunteered for the army.

Poor Mama, he thought. Nothing but trouble all through her life. He brought her pain by volunteering. He made her suffer. Why do folks ostracize her because of her son's act? Now it was Frank's turn to give her pain. No, he could not tell Mama about Frank—not at this time. He must keep it to himself—there was still hope. He must talk to Frank. God, what could he be doing to overlook his supper?

"Mama, let's begin eating. Frank'll be coming in," he said as cheerfully as he could.

"Yes, you shall be late for the meeting," Mama said.

Yes, I must go to the meeting, he thought. I wouldn't miss this for anything. Only the trusted loyalists will be there and we'll form a strong committee.

"Is Frank going tonight?" she asked, as she filled a rice bowl and brought it to the image of Buddha for offering. She clasped her hands together just below her chin and bowed humbly.

For Buddha and in the memory of Papa, he thought.

"No, Mama," he said. She doesn't know yet, he thought. No one has told her about Frank. Damned if I don't see Frank soon.

There was a single light shining in the mess hall as he reached the block. The doors were closed tightly and he had difficulty in gaining entrance. Near the platform were grouped twenty or more youths. They greeted Hiro.

"You're just in time to become a member of the planning committee," Tad Aihara said, making room for him.

"If I can be of any use I'll accept the responsibility," he said and nodding to his friends, he greeted them one by one. There was Yosh Yoshida, Tack Saiki, and Susumu.... George Sato, the leader and chairman of the meeting, resumed.

"Our purpose here tonight is to form a nucleus that will surpass the opposition. They will use force; already their brutal tactics are weaning away our fellow volunteers. This is partly due to our disorganization. We must have force—not just a credo and individual aims. Let us not scatter and waste our energy. Let us unite—and we are the ones who must create that unity."

"That's it, boys," Tad Aihara cried. "Let's get together and work like a team. We need support. Let's make that support strong—that's our job and goal."

Voices of approval came quickly. "Now you're talking," said Susumu. "Let's get down to brass tacks. What're the details? What's the plan?"

"We're getting to it," George Sato said. "If I have the full support of this body..."

"You have," Susumu said.

"Wait a minute. I've got something to say." It was Tack Saiki. His face was not smiling now but solemn and stern. He addressed the group though he faced George Sato as he said, "I object to this force-meets-force business. I don't see any sense in fighting them. We're fighting the enemies across the seas. Why should we have a scrap with these Nisei who are demanding civil rights? They're helping us regain our status."

"But they're using strong-arm tactics," cut in Tad Aihara. "We can't sit still and let them knock our men off their feet."

"Who says they're threatening and using clubs?" Tack demanded, studying the group with scrutiny.

"I said so," Tad cried. "They ganged up on my friend last night. His name is Sax Hinode and he's in the hospital."

"That's a lie. How can you be so sure?" retorted a youth named Kurokami. "There's no proof—no evidence. Maybe it was a personal affair."

"I can name a few who belong to that gang, and one of them is here tonight," Tad said coldly.

"Name him," cried Kurokami, bristling. "I dare you to name him."

"Boys, boys! Let's come to order," George Sato cried.

Tack Saiki rose to his feet; his face was greenishly pale and his hands were trembling. "I'm withdrawing from this organization. You're all wrong—and you're sneaky, liars and dirty. You're vainglorious—you're not fighting for the cause of common men. You want cheap honors. You want yourselves to look big before the American public. And by doing this you're double-crossing your Nisei."

"We don't want your kind," Tad said, pointing to the door. "If you're going to stand by your words, you can leave now."

Tack Saiki laughed harshly. "I'll be glad to go. Before I leave I'll warn you that you'd better scrutinize your fine confederates. Maybe you'll have to whitewash some if you're going to hold them."

"Yeah, tell them about a fancy pigeon they got here—a dandy of a stool pigeon," derisively cried Kurokami.

The room was now deadly still but for the pair. Tack Saiki chuckled hoarsely. "You have a dog in your midst. Maybe you don't know what a dog looks like? Well, I'll tell you so your fishy eyes can see straight. A dog is a Japanese who sniffs and smells out the scent. He is a dog, for he can tell what's going on. And he goes to every post, for he has no home. You're lousy with this kind of animal."

"Show these learned gentlemen and patriots an example of this species," Kurokami said, snickering. "Maybe they'll think twice before they do harm to the people. Name one, Tack."

"That's easy," Tack said, preparing to leave the group. "I'll name the biggest dog here. He's got a brother in the other group and this dog is here tonight looking innocent and goody-goody. There he is—Hiro Murata."

For a second Hiro did not grasp the turn of events. He sat still, numbed by the swift surprise accusation. The group stared at him soberly, unaware that Tack Saiki and Kurokami had left the hall.

He heard Tack's loud throaty laughter coming from outside, and then he was aroused. His face reddened; he wanted to run after Tack and bring him back—make him knuckle down and say uncle. But he saw the sober faces about him, waiting for a word from him.

The room chilled with silence. They demanded an explanation; they expected a denial, but would they believe him? "It's a trick—an old game," he said thickly. "Believe me—they want our group to be suspicious of each other. They want disunity and prejudice. I'm not a dog—any more than Tad Aihara is or George Sato. I hope you believe me."

No one spoke for a long time. George Sato cleared his throat but made no comment. Finally Tad Aihara said quietly, "I believe you, Hiro."

The hall, however, remained quiet and the group unresponsive.

He was halfway home when he thought he heard soft footsteps. He sharply looked back and around but no one was in sight.

The road was dark and deserted. He gazed suspiciously into the blackness that was the high school lot. The lights of the barracks on the left seemed remote and alien. He decided to cut into the next block that was well lit. I'll cut through the blocks, he thought.

As Hiro cut to his left at an angle, he had a sinking sensation that something was hovering nearby. He glanced back in time to see a group of dark figures bearing down upon him. He ducked instinctively as a black object swished through the air. A rough hand grabbed the back collar of his shirt and choked him. He swung around with both fists flailing. They hit something soft and flabby, and he heard a grunt.

"Get the sonofabitch!" cursed a voice.

They made a ring about him and closed in. A figure rushed him and he swung. In the same split second his head rang with a blow. A fist smashed his mouth; a head bucked his stomach.

"Come on! Finish him!" He reeled and spat something thick. He kicked and ducked. Taking a few steps backward, he charged suddenly. Breaking through, he almost fell on his knees by the force and impact of his drive.

"Don't let him get away! Get the bastard!"

He ran straight and swiftly. He heard the pounding footsteps and the shouts came nearer. Reaching the row of barracks, he cut sharply into an alley and ran in the opposite direction. At the first block, third block, he did not stop. Then he could go no more. He stopped, his chest heaving for air. He bent forward gasping and coughing.

Then he straightened quickly as he heard voices. In the shadow of the barrack he flattened his figure against the side of the building. The voices went away. He remained rigid and silent for myriads of seconds. Then he slowly and cautiously came out of the shadow.

He could not go home right away. They might be waiting for him. I'll wash up here, he thought, heading for the washroom. Ducking his face and head in the basin filled with warm water, he felt better. He nursed his swollen mouth and cut lips. The side of his head felt as though it would burst, but the bruises weren't too noticeable in the mirror.

Who could they have been? I'd give ten years to learn their identity, he thought as he sat on the bench in the shower room. He did not know the voices. Much too dark to have seen the faces. He smoked pensively. Things will come to a head in a short while. There will be a clash—inevitably. Force will take care of force but intelligence... Intelligent ones like Frank are dangerous. Such a kind ignites wherever he makes an appearance. Yes, he must talk to Frank—before it's too late. Without Frank, they would have nothing but force, and force could be accommodated. He stood up, ground his butt thoroughly and watched men, dripping from the shower, come to the bench. An amused look spread on his face as he noticed the men gingerly wiping themselves dry. We try very hard to be clean outside—very rarely inside.

Now he chose the dark road and evaded light. He walked slowly. After his first baptism with violence, he could laugh in pain, revel in suffering. Now and then he looked up and down the road but there was no fear in his eyes.

We clothe our thoughts, our purposes, our evils, he thought. We all do because we are humans and humans are weak. But there are two dominating forces—one force is, at all times, working to clothe the deeds and misdeeds of men, and the other is, in every conscious minute, seeking to undress the misdeeds and deeds of men.

Now he headed straight for the porch light of his apartment. He was cocksure of himself, unafraid, aggressive and sacrificial—as men of courage are in their soaring moments.

4

He lay quietly on his bed but sleep was not in his eyes. He looked to see if his bedlamp light was bothering his mother in the far corner. Her even breathing assured him that she was sound asleep. Frank was late again. Hiro tossed several times, wondering if his brother would come in soon. He thought, I cannot sleep and I must not. Frank will come in—maybe in ten minutes. He looked at the clock on the shelf. Yes, Frank is due around two A.M.

He rose once again and groped for the water bag that hung by the window sill. Pouring himself a drink, he paused by the barrack window. A clear night sky of Utah waiting for the break of day looked cool and impersonal. He heard someone in the barrack stoking the furnace. Far away he heard a truck passing.

Then he heard the outside door open. He's back, he thought breathlessly. His heart pounded, and he wondered why he was feeling this way. Now, now—now is now. He must conceal his excited tone; he must calm down. Steady, steady.

Then Frank quietly slipped in. He looked at Hiro in his pajamas and nodded apologetically. "Sorry, old man. I must've kept you awake." He noiselessly went to his bed and immediately prepared for bed.

Hiro watched him make a quick change. Now Frank was in his pajamas. He hit his pillows and then rolled back the cover. "Frank," Hiro called softly. "Come here. I have something to say to you."

Frank came over by the stove barefooted. He watched curiously as Hiro fed several lumps of coal into the fire. "What's up, Hiro?" he asked.

Hiro warmed himself by the stove. He went to his chair and brought back cigarettes, offering one to Frank. They smoked quietly. He was cool now, and he abruptly began, "Frank, please give it up. Quit before it's too late."

"I have nothing to give up," Frank said slowly and imperturbably. Then he smiled. "Don't worry your head off, Hiro. There's nothing wrong in what I'm doing."

"You're smearing our name," he said. He burst forth, thinking of Papa in his last days. "Have you forgotten what Papa said to us? Please, Frank, remember his wish."

Frank inhaled slowly. "I do remember Papa's words. I also remember his teachings. He was a man of peace—do not forget his philosophy of harmony. It was his dream that someday there will be harmony among the people of the world. And I am working for that harmony."

"But your attitude is contrary to Papa's love for the United States," protested Hiro. "What good is your work if you destroy it?"

"By fighting for our civil rights I show love for the American way of life, am I not?" asked Frank blandly.

He realized the trend of the conversation but persisted doggedly. His logic began to waver as he met his brother's calm, penetrating eyes. "Why don't you serve your country as millions are doing these days? You aren't any different from the rest of the Americans."

"That's the trouble with the people—the way you let the matter slide away with the attitude: 'Oh well, after this war for sure. But now we must think of our obligations more than our integrity.' So war never ends."

"You didn't answer my question. Why do you refuse to bear arms?"

Frank ground his cigarette against the belly of the stove and poked it through the slot. "I don't like war which kills human beings and brings destruction to mankind. I don't want any part of this war or any other wars, and I'm willing to risk my life and freedom for this conviction."

"But you can't do anything all by yourself. You can't stop fate," Hiro said fervently. "Look, Frank. You're going to hurt Mama with this. Don't you see that your efforts are in vain? You're just a tiny voice in a big flood."

"That's why I'm putting my efforts into our organization—to gather more forces so we'll be powerful enough to be heard."

"But look at your comrades. They're a bunch of insincere opportunists. They're not fighting for what you're upholding."

"They can be of some use," smiled Frank. He added, "Here is our immediate problem—our Nisei position. I'm asking for the privileges that all citizens deserve under the civil rights. You can't deny our strange situation."

Hiro did not reply.

"If we're fighting for freedom so free men can live as equals, then why are we here in the first place? Why must we citizens of the leading democratic nation be ordered behind the barbed-wire fence when we have committed no crime?"

"Look here, Frank," he suggested eagerly and quickly. "Why don't you put this off till the war's over? There'll be a redress when this is all over."

Frank gazed slyly at him as if he were being made sport of. "Uncle Sam usually forgets problems that were magnified during wartime, and when the war is over it is too late. Then he has to take care of the more immediate worries. You'd be buried—you'd be forgotten and deserve no attention."

"Come on, Frank," he pleaded desperately. "For our family's sake— please. Get away from that bunch. Think it over, won't you?"

His brother shook his head and smiled.

"Not any more than you'd want to quit your group. No. It's no go."

"Think it over, Frank. Take a few days to think it over," he said anxiously.

Frank smiled and patted his younger brother on the back. "I won't try to change you, so please respect my view too. We each have a goal. We can't agree. Okay—let it ride. How about shaking hands on it?"

"No, no." He shook his head and attempted to stop Frank. The latter slipped in the bed and yawned sleepily.

"Let's hit the hay, Hiro," he said. "I'm dog tired. Shut off the light."

Reluctantly Hiro switched the light off. He sighed heavily and stretched out in the bed. The room became quiet. A reflection from the fire played on the ceiling. "Frank," he said softly. "Think it over, will you?"

"Oh, lay off, will you?"

5

The day was warm and sunny. The ground had thawed sufficiently for garden work, and now the people frequented themselves at the front. He saw her pottering in her tiny well-kept garden from a distance.

At the sight of her he brightened quickly. Now he walked briskly. His dark hours of the past few days washed away. Keep her eyes; keep her legs; keep her lovely face; keep her personality; keep her spirit; keep her goodness, he vowed fervently. Keep her laughter; keep her smile; keep her love.

A block away he whistled to her. He saw her figure straighten up and then she was running toward him. Keep her gaiety; keep her humor, he thought, and smiled. "Hi, Jean," he called.

"Where have you been the last few days? I thought something happened to you," she cried anxiously, gladly, piquantly. She rubbed his hands tenderly as they slowly approached the house. "I was so worried today I was about to go to your house. Is anything wrong?"

"Nothing, Jean," he said lightly. "Don't worry your pretty little head. You'll get old fast."

They laughed but both sobered quickly. He gazed at her for a trace of sadness and worry. Oh, sweet. How much you are sacrificing for me and how little I give in return, he thought tenderly. If everything could be sweet; if our love could have a Hollywood ending. If things could be honey all the time. If only we could fly with happiness. If we could only erase trouble and worry. Is ours greater and sweeter for the troubles we have?

She guided him away from the house, and he looked questioningly at her. "They're much upset so we better avoid the house," she explained.

"About what?" he asked, half suspecting that he knew what it was. He glanced at the apartment and at that moment a woman appeared on the steps. She stood there looking scorchingly at the pair. He could see her eyes working with venom and hate. Jean saw her and pulled away hurriedly.

"She wants me to part from you. They're ordering me to join them for Tule Lake," she said sadly.

"Are you?" His voice sounded far away and his spirit wavered for a moment. Segregation, segregation, he thought dully. In a few days her parents will leave for Tule Lake. They are repatriates; they are bound for Japan. Must she obey them? Will she go?

"Do you think I would?"

"You would not leave me. Not you—would you?"

"You are not sure?"

"Yes, I'm sure you aren't going, Jean. You're not going."

"I could not sleep last night. One minute I was going. Next minute I was staying with you."

"Jean, say you're staying. Please."

She did not answer readily. They walked down the road, avoiding the trucks as they roared by. The drivers blew their horns at Hiro but the latter did not hear. He was studying her face soberly and quietly.

"When I started thinking of how much they've done for me till now, I couldn't say no. Now with Jack overseas they only have me for future support. How can I say no?"

"Then you did agree to accompany them? Tell me, Jean."

"If my parents and I separate now, we will never see one another again. This will be so, they told me." She looked at him as she added, "But I did not say one way or the other, Hiro. I have not answered."

"You must stay, Jean. What am I going to do if you leave? Don't you see—it means everything to me," he said eagerly, tightening his hold on her hand. "Think of Jack too, Jean. He'll be all alone if you go. Are you going to let a soldier down? Why do you suppose he volunteered for the 442nd Infantry? For you, sweet, and many more like you. This is no time for you to quibble about family obligations. For once, your country claims you more than your blood ties."

"I shall see, Hiro. I'll tell my parents."

"You shall see!" he cried desperately. "You must say no to them. Tell them no—are you going to wreck both of our lives? Do you think they had any regards for your happiness when they repatriated? No, they were selfish. They wanted to see their old folks; they wanted to meet their friends again. How could they leave if they love you and Jack more than anything else?"

"I shall see, Hiro," she said quietly. "I don't want to kill them."

"Let me go to your house and explain it to them," he said eagerly. "Let me try once more."

"No. Not that, Hiro," she protested. "It'll only mean more quarrels. Please don't come to the house anymore. They don't want to see you. Don't you realize how much they hate you? They say you're stealing me away from them."

He nodded tiredly. "Yes, I'm stealing you because you're of age and reason. Don't they realize that you're grown up? Don't they want to see you living your own life? Let me speak to your father then. I know where he works—at the dining hall. I'll take him aside and try to convince him."

Jean shook her head. "No, darling. Leave it to me, please. Don't make it larger than a family affair. I'll let you know."

"When are they leaving for Tule Lake?"

"This coming Wednesday." She sighed heavily. Hiro looked at her. "Am I causing you worry, Hiro? I'm sorry," she said.

He smiled. "I am realizing how much you mean to me."

"I must go back now," she said quickly. "She was packing my clothes for me because I would not see to it."

They cut diagonally across the block. At the mess hall a score of diners were lined up at the main entrance. They wove through the line and headed for home by the shortest route.

"We're late for lunch," he said.

Then she laughed, for the menu called for pork and beans. As they reached the road the mess hall gong rang. First it was one block and then another joined in. Then another, and others chimed their signals concurrently. Soon the people were streaming down the block paths toward the dining hall. Keep these people; keep their appetite and spirit, he thought pitiably. Keep them innocent though cruel they may be at times.

He then lost his thoughts with the awareness of her presence. Keep you; keep you above all, he said to himself. Keep this that you possess now; keep that which you are seeking. Keep me in your world; keep you in my love; keep us in oneness; keep oneness for us all.

She glanced sideways at him and smiled. "Here's where we part. Don't come any further."

"All right," he said reluctantly. Then, suddenly, cheerfully, solemnly he added as if in that moment he were to melt himself into her, "My life depends on you—everything I have, everything I seek."

She did not smile but looked gravely at him for a second. He watched her figure diminish gradually in size till she seemed like a tiny figurine in the world of giants and grotesques.

6

"She's the mother of a dog," he heard.

He did not stop lathering himself. There were several under the shower with him talking among themselves. Apparently they did not hear.

Then he heard the voices in the latrine, but he could not make out who they were. "It is the duty of a parent to guide their children to right thoughts and action, and if a son should go wrong it is criminal that she does not reprimand him." The man was talking loudly.

"She is weak, without spunk," the other guffawed. "Her boy can be put into her eye and yet cause her no pain."

"Too bad her husband is dead. This is the result of an upbringing without a man in the family."

He strained himself to hear more but was unable to grasp the low mutterings that followed. Now he turned on the water and washed himself hurriedly.

If he could only get out of the shower quick enough and learn the identity of those men. They are Issei, he thought madly. What right have they to talk bad about his mother? What do they know about his family and what business is it of theirs? They don't want trouble for themselves but make trouble for others.

You volunteer and it becomes everybody's business. You volunteer and they think you've become a man-killer. You volunteer and they think you're stupid and foolish for jumping into the fire. You are hated and abused by the young who hate to go to war. You are accused of reopening the draft for Nisei and so you are the devil. You are seeking personal glory and commissioned ranks; you are the patented hero,

163

American-made. You are sending others to butcher themselves to hell and gone. You are the despised who are diseased with the cancer to make war, to prolong war, to glorify war.

You are not a man of feelings; you are an automaton. You have no union with the people's thoughts and aspirations; you have not communed with anyone but with the selfish self. Yes, you are the traitor of your ancestors. You are the damned; you are the purveyor of evil; you are the carrier of mankind's pus.

When he came out of the shower no one was in the washroom. There was a peaceful air in the room, a lull that brought restlessness into his lean frame. He looked in the mirror—there was once an innocent, naive youngster in you, his image said. He was once pure as humans come; he was a child, once helpless, once a being who was all for the taking without a conscious greed. He was once an animal who did not know the game nor the man-made rules; he was the believer of yes for yes and no for no.

And now look at you—you are crafty; you are smart; you have fists; you have hate; you have brutal strength; you have lust; you have greed. You are green in the game but learning mighty fast. You are picking up knowledge—higher learning, and profitable, from the street. Better go easy there, Hiro Murata, citizen of the United States and of the earth. Think rationally, kid. Don't raise your blood pressure over little matters. There is to come the bigger things in your life. Store up your energy for your day of days. When it comes, shoot the works.

And about the conscience, young fellow. Who made you as you are today? Was it yourself alone or did time and environment make you? You are you now. You are wrong in many ways, and you are right sometimes. Say to the public, "Time made this man!" But have the guts, little man, when you come face to face with yourself to admit, hereafter, I become responsible for myself because I have eyes to see.

Go all the way, rookie. Follow through. Don't hesitate. You wouldn't hesitate if you're taking a cut at the ball, would you? You wouldn't stop to study whether you're biting at a bad one, would you? You would rest on your judgment, good or bad. Is it not so? You either swing or you don't. Life is a game too, and life is full of mistakes, old man—without and within. Don't get gray and old over mistakes—mistakes make you,

you know, if you have taken a cut cleanly. Yeah, man, keep cool for now. Ask for time. The rest will come to you whether you like it or not.

Wearing his Topaz-made wooden clogs Hiro now walked homeward. The south wind picked up the loose surface dust and skyward it swirled. He followed its pattern with a detached thought. Last year I would have exclaimed and damned the place. Now I lift my eyes for the direction of its path and see nothing startling about it. I am callous and blasé; therefore, I have grown.

His mother was waiting for him by the doorway, standing empty-handed and nervously.

"What's the matter, Mama? Isn't it time to get supper?" he asked, noting her unusual behavior.

"We're going to the mess hall tonight for supper," she said decisively. Her voice, though faltering, had a purpose.

"Okay," he agreed. Then he could not ignore her agitation. "Why, Mama? Are there some special doings in this block?"

"No. I am going there to give the block people a piece of my mind. I want to speak to them—explain to them that what we do is our affair. I want them to understand that we are not the kind of folks to stand for insults."

Oh, oh, he thought, knowing well her fury once aroused. Not now, Mama. Hold it a little longer. Allow me the opportunity. "No use, Mama. They talk behind our backs. Let them have their day. We'll have ours."

"I want criticism stopped," she cracked sharply.

Her obstinate temper cut his protest short. Has the time come already? he asked. Ready or not, we are it. Is this the time to prick the boil?

It was a normal day for the average diners, but for the Muratas it was a special one. They stood in the line with the rest in cafeteria style as they went past the serving counter. Some looked at them curiously but the majority was not aware of their presence.

His mother's eyes glittered with cold fury as he nervously talked to her. She is preparing herself for the occasion, he thought. She is steeling herself. Jesus Christ, it's going to be uncomfortable sitting in there. She has the gumption; she will spill everything. What a woman. Boy, these people will have a come-down.

He chuckled to himself, picturing the relaxed faces stiffening with the outburst. It could be funny; it could be nothing but funny to him at this time.

It was a meatless lunch as usual. They went to their table, their plates filled with carrots, potatoes, and onions cooked in shoyu sauce. On each table was a plate of lettuce salad. They took strong tea.

Before they had scarcely wetted their mouths, his mother approached the block manager, who made announcements for his block. Hiro saw him nodding his assent to Mama's request, and then he paid attention to his food.

The block manager rapped the triangle for attention. Here goes, he said to himself. He could see Mama standing beside him, fairly bursting with fire.

"Mrs. Murata wishes to address you people. You have the floor, Murata-san," said the block manager.

She was fairly cold and unprepared when she began. Her voice was trembling and high-pitched. "I have something to say to you folks. It has been on my mind for quite a while. I always like to keep matters straight, and if I should happen to hurt some of your feelings it is because you have wormed into my family's affair."

Hiro sat chilled in his seat. He squirmed and kept his eyes on the food. The room was still.

"My son, as you well know, volunteered for the United States Army. As this is the sore subject which alienates you people from us, I shall enter into our private affair once and for all. If you cannot understand us after hearing me—then—then we can do nothing to bridge our differences.

"I have heard many times, both directly and indirectly, the harsh criticism coming our way. And why do we receive this treatment? Simply because my son here volunteered for the Army. Before that, you counted us as one of you. Now, we are ostracized.

"As a mother I shall relate to you how I felt when he volunteered. When my son told me that he had volunteered for combat duty I broke down. As a mother I was thinking in terms of our personal life. I raised him so he could, in my old age, give me comfort and support. I did not want him to die. I wanted him; I needed him. It was cruel that he must go."

Now Hiro looked at his mother unashamedly. Her eyes were clear and piercing as she commanded attention. A hush fell over the people as she paused.

"Do not for one minute think that my boy plunged into this with youthful fervor. My friends and priests vainly advised him against leaving his mother behind. For days and weeks my boy withstood these men—thoroughly convinced of his convictions. And what is that—this conviction which some of you are attempting to destroy in a Nisei? He is as much a Nisei as you are an Issei. It may be unusual for an Issei to volunteer but it certainly is not when a Nisei does."

His eyes were glistening; drops of warm tears fell on his lap. He did not raise his head. Mother, Mother, he whispered. I did not think you understood.

"And what are his reasons for volunteering—volunteering from a concentration camp, if you consider it so? What makes him risk his hide when he does not have to? He volunteered, fellow people, because he does not know any country but this land. He does not know Japan; he does not know England nor Russia nor China. He does know the place where he was born and raised. He does know its familiar way of life, and don't tell me that that is unimportant. The way some of you Issei speak adoringly of your mother country shows what the early ties could do to individuals. Some of you cannot forget Japan, and here I mean the Japan of your childhood days—the cherry blossom festivals, the holidays, the beautiful lakes and mountainsides, the quaint villages, the dragonflies and the cicadas in the summer evenings.

"So when my son responded to his country's call, he had memories and visions—just like you. He too has the smells, the sights, the flavors, the music that possess him. He is you—he represents you who are living and dying here. And those of you who are smiling amusedly because you are not going to die here but return to Japan, I ask you—why did you come to America? What was your purpose? Why did you remain? Answer me these with reason."

My mother is illiterate; she did not have a formal education, he thought. But she knows a hell of a lot more than these squirming gentlemen and ladies. She's having a field day here.

"My friends persuaded vainly. My son was unmoved. They told him

167

that if he joined the Army he was going to die. Then he told them; my boy did. He said, 'I am going all right but I'm not volunteering to die—I'm a soldier who wants to live. Because I want to live I am volunteering.' He and those who volunteered want to live. They want themselves to live; they want their families to live; they want their families' families to live."

I am glad; I am glad for this day; I am glad that there was the time and place for all that occurred on account of my volunteering, he thought.

"Now, we are returning to the petty things—to the matters which make life unpleasant for us. If you still can't agree with us, will you please keep it to yourself? It is not your business if my son wishes to serve his country. It is he who is risking life—not you. And if he believes it is worthwhile, you or anyone else have no right to stop him—not even his mother.

"And mark my words, folks. These boys who serve for us, the people, they will be remembered in the annals of this country. They will be remembered as those who led the crusade for freedom and peace in behalf of their people."

There was not a sound in the room as his mother returned to her table. He watched her sit down and peck at her food. Their plates were heaping full when they rose to go.

He walked with his head high. He could see their eyes following them. Yes, she is my mother, and I am the son who volunteered. Whatever she said, now I am responsible, his eyes and bearing said. If there is further ado, look me up. Gradually the clatter of knives and forks filled the air, but there was little laughter and talk.

He and Mama were first to leave the dining hall.

7

As he approached the canteen he saw them out in the front. It was the same bunch that he had bumped into that night in the middle of the road. He could see his brother Frank holding the group's rapt attention. There was John Tabe and Kurokami and Tack Saiki.

Then he saw Yosh Yoshida in the group. What was he doing with them? And where had he been keeping himself lately? Yosh had not been to the house for days.

"Hi, Yosh," he called as he neared them. Now the group moved away, talking animatedly. He waited as Yosh stopped and slowly came back. He nodded to others as they glanced back and stopped.

"Long time no see," Hiro said.

Yosh did not smile. His face was an impenetrable mask. "Sorry, Hiro," he said lamely. He nodded in the direction of the group. "They're waiting for me—I've got to be going. See you later."

"Wait," Hiro said, putting his hand on his shoulder. "Let them go, Yosh. Come and have a Coke with me."

"Hurry up, Yosh," called Frank.

"They're calling me. I'll see you again," Yosh said hurriedly.

"What's the matter, Yosh?" he asked, bristling. "You don't like my company? Is that it?"

Yosh did not answer.

"So you prefer that bunch to me, eh? And I thought we understood each other."

"No, it's not that, Hiro."

"What is it then?"

"Shake your leg, Yosh," Frank said impatiently. "We haven't much time before supper."

John Tabe beckoned with his hand. "Come on, Yosh."

"Listen, Hiro," Yosh said. "I've got some business right now. Honest—they're waiting for me. So long."

He still gripped Yosh's shoulders. "Did you fall for Frank's line?" he said coldly.

Yosh evaded his eyes. He jerked away and fairly ran to the waiting group.

Looking at them go down the street Hiro caught Tack Saiki's smug triumphant leer as a parting shot. You must stop this, he said, staring at the broad back of his brother. You must stop this.

Now he turned back. His head burned with a helpless, smoldering fury. Again, again, he thought. One more down. What are we doing about it? Who sees this that I see? I must tell it to someone; I must have someone to help me.

He walked straight to Tad Aihara's apartment. They stood on the porch and chatted. "How is our group doing?" he asked offhand. "Do you know, Tad?"

"We're doing okay," Tad said lightly. "We've added a few more volunteers in the last two days."

"But have we gained in number?" he said persistently. "Can you account for our old members?"

"Sure, why not? They're old standbys."

"Did you know that we lost Yosh Yoshida to them?" he asked quietly.

"You're kidding, Hiro. He wouldn't do a thing like that."

"If you won't believe me, you're going to have a surprise coming."

"Did he go over—honest?" Tad said, now serious. When Hiro nodded, he whistled softly. "This is getting serious."

Hiro sat on the porch rail. He offered a cigarette to Tad. They smoked silently. "What good will new additions be if we can't hold them—especially the old members? When the old ones go confidence and spirit go too."

Tad nodded, puffing rapidly. "I'd like to catch hold of John Tabe," he said. "He's behind all this. He's one guy I'd like to see get it."

"He's not the one, Tad. There's a bigger one than him," Hiro said quietly.

"John Tabe is the chairman, you know. He's on every committee."

"But he isn't the leader."

"Who is, then?"

"My brother Frank," he said softly. "He's the one we must stop."

Tad Aihara did not look up immediately. He flipped his dying cigarette to the ground. Then he took out his Chesterfields and offered them to Hiro. He struck a match for both of them. "What are you going to do?"

Hiro shook his head slowly. He was honest with himself. He did not know what to do; he did not see how one was to do what he must do. But he knew for certain that he must meet whatever is to come, whenever the day. And then he would have to act precisely, swiftly, wisely.

"Count on me," Tad said slowly. "Whatever you do I'll back you."

He nodded and smiled back. He could trust this young one. He was solid; his word was trust. "I'll need your help," he said simply.

I must ready myself, he thought, walking homeward. It cannot come too soon. I am ready for that. But what if there is no crisis, no issue, that I can act upon? Suppose it is like the low rolling hills of the plains? Suppose it does not present visible obstacles? That is the catch.

Frank is where others are not, he knew. Now you see him, now you don't. That is, you are unable to follow him all the time. Frank will give you a pain in the neck. Already he has. He has brains; he can talk; he has sincerity; he works. Frank can win where others fall in defeat; Frank can see weakness in himself and strength in the opposition as he wins.

What is to come will come, he warned himself. But I am thinking, should I meet him on his home grounds where he is strongest or should I choose the time and circumstance? If I should choose, then I must lead. That is the catch again.

In the evening a sharp wind came whipping from the mountain. It rattled the makeshift windows and ripped the tar-roofing paper from the barracks. Frank was home early for once but there was little merrymaking. They ate their meals silently, and now the mother made no effort in pleasant talk. When she went out with the panful of soiled dishes to the laundry room, the boys were self-conscious.

It was Hiro again who tried. "Frank, you must stop it. You must agree to quit this time."

A trace of a smile appeared in Frank's face and it quickly disappeared.

"I believe you know what I mean."

"And if I say no as usual?" coolly asked Frank.

Hiro shut up momentarily. He looked at his brother. "You must say yes this time," he said slowly.

"If I said yes to you and then went on acting no, would you like it?" Frank said.

"No. Not from you."

"Then I must say no to you."

"Is that final? Will you ever change? Will you ever sacrifice yourself for the family? Will you?"

"No."

Hiro went to the window. His eyes absently watched the sweeping wind drive into the dust and raise it sky high. Almost immediately there was the pitter-patter tapping of cloudburst on the roof.

"Are you sore about today?" Frank asked from a faraway distance.

"No," he said. "If he's weak and you're strong, that is not your fault."

Frank smiled. "Then you understand," he said gladly. He added quickly. "Don't tell Mama about this—I'm moving away from here tonight. Tack Saiki invited me over to bunk with him and I said okay."

"Why don't you stay home?" he asked slowly.

"I don't want to quarrel with you, Hiro. If I stay here much longer we might get nasty with each other, and I don't want that to happen." He quickly went to the bed and began bundling up his nightclothes and pillow in a duffle bag. "Why should we quarrel?"

Hiro watched him pack. "We can live together without quarreling."

"No, that's impossible. I will bring you embarrassment, and I will bring you anger."

"We should not be afraid of quarreling. Maybe we can agree after quarreling."

"But we have tempers, Hiro. And we're humans. I don't like quarrels. And why should we present ourselves with a showdown? I'm not fighting you any more than you are fighting me. This issue is more than just you and me. So why should we quarrel?"

"Okay," Hiro said finally.

Frank came over and patted his back. "Tell Mama I'm just visiting Tack Saiki. Don't let her worry."

Hiro nodded. He left Frank's side and went to the window. The cloud-burst had stopped and now the alley between the barracks was a lake of unabsorbed rainwater. "Will you shake hands?" Frank said, smiling.

They gripped hands tightly, and then Frank turned sharply on his heels and left the apartment.

8

It was nine o'clock in the evening when Hiro reached his block. Though he neared his barrack his eyes did not immediately detect it. The gravel path between the barracks and the mess hall was dark. Funny. Block lights should be on, he thought.

All along the line there was not a single light. Once he thought he saw a shadow emerge from the other end of the barrack. He stopped curiously and then, reassuring himself, proceeded to his apartment.

"Just in time, Hiro," Mama said, pouring coffee into the cups. "Look, I have something special for you."

"What is it, Mama?" His eyes brightened. These late snacks always cheered him. Now the outside world was far away. He was home, and Mama had a special snack for him. He lifted the cover cloth and peeked in. He smacked his lips as Mama watched him happily. "You're spoiling me, Mama. What's the occasion?"

"Providence comes unexpectedly and abundantly," she said and smiled. "These sandwiches and olives came from Jean. She made them for us. And these doughnuts my mess hall friends brought. Those bananas are from our dear friends, the Hashimotos in Indiana. And this pineapple pie I happened to order at the pastry shop today because you like pies."

"Boy, oh boy," he cried, rubbing his hands and quickly sitting down. "This is luck or do we deserve all this? Hurry up, Mama. Let's celebrate."

Then he thought of the ginger ale he had saved and brought it out. "We're in style tonight." He poured it into two tumblers and giving one to her, he raised his. "For the good that is deserving to all."

175

His mother watched him gladly and followed suit. "How did the meeting go?" she asked.

"It could have been better," he said, biting into a double-decker sandwich. "Try the sandwiches, Mama—they're really good. When did Jean come over?"

"Just before dark."

"Did she leave a message?"

"No. She stayed but a few minutes."

"How did she look? Did you notice how she carried herself?" he asked. "Did she seem upset?"

"No. She looked calm. She looked pretty, if that's what you're asking me."

He could see her standing in front of his mother, chatting fluently in Japanese. She would have the white scarf about her head, and she would be wearing her beige coat. "What did she talk about?"

She laughed heartily. "She chatted about the weather and about what she must do tonight when I asked her in."

"About what?"

"Oh, the inconsequential things that a woman must do around the house." She gazed at him amusedly and knowingly. "Why do you ask, son?"

"Her parents are leaving for Tule Lake the day after tomorrow," he said. "I asked her to stay."

She smiled. "She'll remain behind."

"How do you know, Mama?" he asked quickly. "Did she tell you that?"

"No, son. But I know. She'll stay."

"I wish I were sure," Hiro said. He added doubtfully, "How can you tell how she feels?"

"Because I can see through her," she said, smiling confidently. "She'll stay."

"I hope you're right, Mama."

"I am right," she said. "You are not eating, Hiro. Do not worry but eat. You cannot be a good soldier with just skin and bones. Eat hearty."

"I'm eating, Mama. I like to eat."

"Eat well, son. Eat well for the future. Did you acquire new recruits today?"

"Yes, a few," he said. "There was one boy's parents I felt sorry for today. This boy is eighteen and he volunteered against their wishes. They threatened to disown him, but today he joined us. Then there was a youth who begged us to help him because the bullies in his block worked on him. They heard about his action and now they're laying for him."

"What are you doing to protect these young boys?" she asked anxiously. "They must not be wronged; they must be given help."

"Tonight we decided to go around in groups. After dark we are never to be alone but in pairs at least. If we have late meetings then we are to double up. I've arranged with Tad Aihara so he'll come over and stay with us after late meetings."

"That is good," she said, pouring coffee again. "Caution is a weapon that costs nothing."

"That is so, Mama," he replied. "Will you cut me another piece of that pie?"

"The young can be intimidated easily," she went on, serving him the pie. "They are not weak but can be led like sheep sometimes."

Hiro nodded his head, wiping his mouth luxuriously with his napkin and resting back comfortably. There was a moment of silence, when the ticking of the clock came clear across the room. Then came a crash that split and drummed the room with reverberations.

A rock, of a shotput size, rolled to the floor before the glass shattered in all directions. "Duck under, Mama!" cried Hiro, pulling her away. "Come on!"

Before they were across the room, countless objects rained into the room from every window. He dragged her under the bed, and they covered their heads with their arms. They heard the dishes crashing to the floor. The bridge table toppled over.

Then he thought of the light. He darted for the switch and reached it. Just as the darkness covered the room, his head was hit by a stinging rock. His arm felt numb as the hollow sound of a pipe rang as it went bouncing to the floor. A lamp near the window crashed and then there was a splashing sound as if a paper bag filled with water went plop to the floor. Instantly there was a strong, stinking smell that reached his nostrils. Dung, his mind cried.

Now his anger rose, and he tore to the window. He saw the fading figures in the distance, their laughter coming faintly.

Then he heard the excited voices outside his door. There was the pounding on his door, and he dazedly stood without answering.

"Someone is at the door, Hiro," Mama said, crawling out from her hiding. "Put on the light, son." Her voice was cool and strong. She moved to the center of the room and finally found the switch.

"What's wrong in here? What's happened? Murata-san!" cried an excited voice. It was their neighbor. Then he opened the door as the blaze of light went on.

Hiro went to his mother's side. "This is the end; this is the finish. We're ruined!"

"Is that so?" countered his mother. "Who says so? Is this Hiro Murata speaking?"

He did not answer. He looked dazedly at the disorder. He could not answer—answer with misery nor with defeat.

9

Now Hiro was certain that she was staying. His mother had been right. Jean walked beside him, clinging to his arm possessively as if he were the only link to life for her. He looked down and smiled at her serious, solemn face. He began chuckling. All the way to the gatehouse he laughed softly and endlessly.

"What's so funny, darling?" she asked puzzledly. "What strikes you as comical?"

He laughed all the more. "I am crazy. Never mind me, Jean. I'm so happy I've got to laugh. I was so miserable the last few days. I am breaking out now. Now I laugh because it doesn't matter whether I am happy or miserable. Do you get it?"

"No. Are you referring to us?"

"Yes and to other matters—all the problems under the sun."

"I do not understand," she said. "Do you laugh because everything has become cheap? Even our love?"

"No, sweet," he said gently. "No, I laugh because I do care—but in a different way, a more sober outlook. You will begin to live with a more matured man. You will see."

"I don't understand but I hope I will."

"You will, Jean," he said as they neared the gatehouse. "I am young but have tasted defeats many times. So many in many ways that now I am not hurt by defeats. I'm not afraid of failures and I realize the limit of myself."

She did not reply but clung to his side.

"Do you know that you're going to marry a limited man, sweet?" he said, smiling. "He has reached his limits. He knows his limitations, and he isn't going beyond its border."

"At least, you can't frighten me."

"No. You frighten me more often."

"Do I? Do I truly?"

"Yes," he said. "Sometimes I do not understand you, and that scares me."

"I did not understand you a minute ago and yet I was not frightened."

He laughed. "I told you you were braver and stronger. You understand me as I am to you, and that you know perfectly more than I do myself. And what you do not understand about me does not affect you. Is it not so?"

"Yes," she agreed. "But I am now curious. What are you going to do now that you are a limited man. What good shall I see from my limited man?"

He chuckled. "Must you know, Jean?"

"I want to know."

"You will not understand."

"I will. Tell me quickly."

"All right. By realizing my limitations I will travel unlimited within the limits."

"I do not understand."

"See, I told you."

"Tell it to me slowly, or, better, put yourself in. Don't be general."

"Some other time, sweet. Forget it," he said. "We're supposed to go walking and enjoy the freedom outside of the barbed wire fence."

"Tell me."

"Stubborn." She pinched him, and he jumped away. "That hurts. Let up, Jean. I'll explain."

He rubbed his arm gingerly. His eyes twinkled merrily. The sun was bright and the sky clear. The recent rains awakened green shoots from sagebrushes. "Whenever things went wrong with me I tightened up. I was full of nerves; I was shaky; I was afraid—afraid of death, of failure, of obstacles. Now I can laugh. See what I mean? I am not being cocky but I laugh. I laugh because I can live and I laugh because I must die."

The girl slowly nodded her head. "I think I can grasp a little of your words."

"A little at a time is okay. Some are unable and unwilling," he said and laughed. "We have a lifetime before us. Now let's go picnicking."

"But I did not bring lunch," she said quickly.

"I was only kidding. We'll return by noon."

At the gatehouse they waited for the guard to inspect their identification card. They walked through the gate and out. "Where you going?" the soldier on duty asked in a friendly tone.

"We're going walking," Hiro said.

"Better be back by sundown," the soldier said, grinning.

"We'll be back by lunchtime," he said. "We can't go very far without eating."

"You can go far when in love."

They laughed and walked away slowly. The sun bore down on them, their faces and backs warm and perspiring. They looked at the green fields with fresh interest.

"Looks nice, doesn't it?" he said. "Green surroundings—makes one feel living and growing."

"It does, Hiro." Her eyes looked rested. "Doesn't that green strike you as odd? That green looks strange, or is it my eyes? It looks artificial."

"It is not as green as we were used to but now it is as green as we can see."

"Oh, Hiro," cried Jean, piqued. "Why do you make it so difficult?"

"You're to blame."

"Me? What do you mean?"

"You make me giddy."

"Oh, hush."

Now Hiro took off his jacket. They stood and watched many semi-trailers leave the camp, approach them, and then roar past them. They were heavily loaded with crates piled higher than their stakes. "Bound for Tule Lake," he said.

"Yes, for Tule," she said sadly. "Only a few more hours and they're leaving here forever."

"Maybe you should go back and be with your parents today," he suggested, watching her face work with emotions. "Maybe we ought to go back."

"No, no," she cried quickly. "It'll make things worse. Better that I don't see them till parting time. I can't stay home."

"Why must they go?" He put his arm around her waist. "I feel sorry for them. Today I feel guilty."

"It's their heart's choice," she said, steeling herself. Her eyes were brave rather than cold. "They have no regrets. Why should I have any now?"

"Are you sure that you want to stay behind with me? You won't regret it later?" he said, anxious for her. He watched her nod emphatically.

"Yes, yes," she said almost fiercely.

"I hope I can make you happy. I hope everything will turn out okay."

"It will. It will," she cried. "Why do you sound hesitant?"

"Our heads may rock with trouble ahead. Maybe our life will not be smooth and rosy. I don't want to give you a fancy picture."

"I know," she said, unnerved but patient. "I know. Do you think I would stay if I were afraid and unsure of myself and you?"

"Then the road is clear." He held her tighter without answering her question. In the distance he heard the noon siren. Now I am hungry, he thought, chuckling at the thought of it. He looked at her and added, "Are you a little afraid—just a wee bit afraid?"

She studied his face and, finding no jocular vein, soberly answered, "Yes, I'm afraid—frightened of the little world we're making. You wanted that confession out of me, didn't you?"

He playfully squeezed her hard. "Yes, my little sweet. Now you make me glad I'm alive."

"Is that so?"

"Yes. Your limited man is happy."

10

At George Sato's mess hall the planning committee members met on the emergency problem. Sooner or later it was coming, Hiro thought, and now it's here before we know it.

"I want to see some action taken," Susumu demanded to the group. "What are we organized for? For tea and chitchat? I want action."

George Sato, the chairman, looked gravely at the members. "We must not antagonize the other group. We mustn't be rash and emotional, fellows."

"Do we have to be nice to those bastards?" Susumu cried. "What for? They're gorillas. They're asking for no quarter. Why the hell should we be hoity-toity to them?"

"I was approached by their group and they wish a compromise with us," George Sato said.

"You can't trust 'em," warned a voice in the room.

"Tell them to go to hell," Tad Aihara said. "They got a nerve putting up a proposition like that."

"Sure nice of them to invite us," Hiro said bitterly. He turned to George Sato. "It's about time we do something about it."

"I'm not for it," George Sato cried. "I don't want bloodshed here."

"We want action," Tad said. "I don't want any more of this mushy stuff. I propose force."

"I second the motion!" prompted Susumu. He glanced at the group for more approval.

"Yes, we're with you fellows," Sax Hinode said. "Aren't we, fellows?"

A unanimous chorus replied.

George Sato rose slowly to his feet. His face turned red but his eyes were steady. "It seems that I am the only dissenting one in the group. It is appropriate that I step down from chairmanship. Therefore, I shall resign at this time."

"You're staying with the committee?" Hiro asked curiously.

The room became silent as the group waited for George Sato's reply.

"Yes, I'll remain on the committee," he said quietly.

"I nominate Tad Aihara for chairman!" Susumu cried immediately.

"I second the motion!" Sax Hinode said.

"I move that the nomination be closed," Hiro said quickly.

"I second the motion!" Susumu cried happily.

"Tad Aihara is our new chairman of the committee!" shouted Hiro.

The noise subsided a little. When Tad rose to accept the chairmanship, he was met with a wholehearted attention.

"Thanks, fellows. I appreciate your support. I hope I can fill the bill," he said simply. "Hereafter, I'll have to call for your help, and I know you'll be around to assist me."

"You bet!" cried several. "If you want bruisers we got 'em! Just let us know!"

"Thanks," he said. "When the time comes for force I'll call on you. But just now we've got to stop the opposition's most powerful weapon. That's Frank Murata. Our important question is what to do with Frank's influence. He's doing more damage than their bruisers, and we must do something about it before anything else."

The room became still. No one looked at Hiro. Their attention was on Tad. "Well, I have an idea," he continued. "I'm going to ask Hiro to try his luck with Frank. More than anyone else here, he is most capable for this job. I know he can solve it if anyone can. What do you say, Hiro? Will you accept the job?"

Hiro cleared his dry throat. "I'll try. I've been trying all this time to stop Frank but failed. Leave it to me a little longer."

"Is it okay, fellows?" Tad asked the group.

"Hiro's the man for the job," Susumu agreed heartily.

11

He watched them from the edge of the crowd. They were now weeping unashamedly—Jean and her mother. They did not speak but clung to each other, wiping their red eyes with handkerchiefs. He saw the mother's friends come and go as they bowed farewell and wept.

In a few minutes the car was to arrive at the block for the segregants. He saw several large families readying themselves. The little children sorrowfully shook hands with their newly-made friends. The poor kids, he thought. They must obey their parents for better or worse. They have no choice. They have no voice.

As the crowd milled about he shifted to the center of the lot. He could see Jean and her mother circled by their friends. In a few minutes this will be all over, he thought, gloating in spite of the scene. I shall have her all to myself.

The people jostled him and he moved into the shadow of the latrine building. He did not wish to lose her in the crowd. He must meet her as soon as possible. Then swiftly, in a moment, he saw the face. It was the face of her father filled with such vicious hatred and venom, he backed away as if to ward off the fangs.

"Devil! Sucker of human blood!" the man screamed.

As he fled, weaving and bobbing through the mob, he heard the cry. "Thief! Devil of this earth! Devil with two horns!"

Several men in the crowd looked at him as he scurried past. As he reached the fringe of the mob, he paused and glanced back. His face was pale in the sunlight. He could not see her father but walked away. This is hell. Why do I run? Am I the sonofabitch? You are running away, Murata. Is that the way of a volunteer? Where are your guts?

Slowly, then, his color returned to his face. His ears turned pink and his eyes smarted. His nose ran. The goddam bastard, he cried, his anger rising slowly, strongly. I could wring his neck! I could exterminate him. But why should I? Why?

Rounding the latrine building he crossed to the other side of the block. From behind a nook of an enclosed porch he gazed at the last minute scene. Now Jean was lost in the crowd. As the bus cut through the gathering it was immediately swallowed by the milling mob.

You could be violent and get no place, he thought. You must be smart like Frank. You must time yourself. Timing counts a lot, my boy. You must work with time. You must be ready; you must be at the peak of efficiency at the momentous time. You must jive with time. Okay. Patience, my boy. Remember that night at your apartment? You have not forgotten, have you? *Boy, if I could only trace those hoodlums!* Remember that other time when they meant to sack you? Remember? Remember well. You are the butt now. You are the receiver of foul names. They spite you for what you have done. *What have I done?* You have accomplished nothing and yet they have you on the rug. They remember you well now. *Remember me well tomorrow.* You're finished, through, according to them. They know you. They sized you. Not by a long shot, eh? They do not know you, bub. You will take knocks; you will take jibes; you will absorb beatings. They do not know this in you: You will not stand for it when they come to crush your spirit. *Yep, I am the bub who takes his spirit straight.* You need spirit. Spirit is you. Without spirit you are not you.

He heard the roar of the motor. He saw the flutterings of handkerchiefs and the waving hands. In his ears rang the shouts of farewell. In his nostrils entered the exhaust fumes as the bus shot out of the block.

12

As Hiro and Tad walked home together late in the night, they saw a lone figure approaching them on the road. He was silhouetted against a block light, and apparently the person was not aware of them.

"Who is that? He looks familiar," Tad asked Hiro, straining forward apprehensively.

He knew the figure instantly. The familiar gait was unmistakable. "It's Frank. No one but Frank," he said.

"All alone too. That's very rare nowadays," Tad said with wonder.

Now they watched him with interest. Hiro stopped and waited and Tad did likewise. They could talk to him, he thought. For once, they would not be bothered by his stooges. They could talk freely; they could act.

"Hi Frank," Tad said casually.

"Oh, hello, boys," Frank said, surprised. He gazed at them as if they were at a great distance. "Out late, aren't you?" he added for want of talk.

"We're going home after a conference," he said, his thoughts wandering. Now I would not be safe alone at this hour but you are, his mind said, gazing at Frank. *You* can move without worry but I can't.

Tad broke the silence. "I hear you got your pre-induction physical call, Frank. You're going to Fort Douglas, aren't you?"

"Sorry to disappoint you fellows but I'm not," he said, smiling.

"I heard about it from the Selective Service officer," Tad said grimly. "You're going to get into trouble. You have no case against the draft."

"I know. I know all about it."

If he were not my brother and I could do it, he thought. It could be an easy solution—if I only could. No more trouble then. It could be

187

easily done; it would work.

"And you're going to stick out your neck?" Tad said. "Why don't you call it off? Think it over, Frank."

Frank chuckled, laying his hands on their shoulders. "Come on, fellows. Let's go to the latrine—I'll show you my letter of protest to the local board. It won't hurt you to see what's wrong with me. Maybe you can help me."

Tad looked at Hiro with an agreeable nod. "Let's see it, Frank. You must have something there."

He is free with his thoughts. He doesn't care who knows his attitude, he thought. That is bad. When is this going to end? How to end? Oh, how to see it through.

They walked three abreast to the nearest washroom. They entered the room empty but for one Issei who quickly left after washing his false teeth.

The pair watched Frank take out a legal-size envelope and carefully unfold the letter. "This is the copy—the apology of my attitude."

Tad took the letter and silently read it. Hiro studied his face for a sign of disapproval. He could not fathom him. When Tad finished reading he handed the letter to Hiro without a comment.

It must be disappointing, he thought. Tad would make a crack; he would be quick with a retort.

"How does it sound to you?" Frank asked cheerfully.

Tad nodded his head. "Okay, if you believe it. But where will it get you? No place but pains and worry for yourself. What do you want?"

"I want man to live peacefully with one another, and whenever a problem should arise, it should be solved by civil methods." He studied their faces to see if they understood. "If individuals can comply to the national laws, why cannot nations comply with universal laws?"

"Don't you think that our present war is a process toward that goal?" asked Tad. "And another thing—what is our universal laws that you're speaking of? Isn't that another evolutionary attainment from this struggle? Why not join the movement? It's here—here to stay for all of us."

"You're wrong there, Tad," Frank said quickly. "Remember the ideals of our last world war? What happened to it? Why did this war start when we had such high-sounding philosophy? You fellows think fate is stronger than man's will. Well, I don't. If every man in the world would realize this senseless butchery of fellow beings and refuse to bear arms or to perform noncombat duties, then this war would die quickly in a day or two. If only every man would realize the opportunity to end this non-sense!"

"If only! You're thinking of the impossible!" Tad added grimly, "We will have war until we reach the zenith of our process. You'd have to wait, Frank. Now isn't the time—you're way ahead of time. You're a man in a million, and what can you do alone?"

"That's right, Frank," Hiro cut in eagerly. "Why don't you wait for the right time?"

Frank waved away the suggestion. "The right time will never come unless you go out and meet it. I'm ready for anything. Why should I wait now? If I wait I'll have time on my hands. No, I'm convinced, boys. You can't change me nor can I change you."

Tad shrugged his shoulders resignedly. He tapped Hiro on the arm. "Well, let's go to sleep. Think it over, Frank—for Hiro's sake."

Frank shook his head, his smile slowly spreading over his entire face. "Cut it out, fellows. Waste of time. Here, Hiro. Give me the letter, will you?"

"But I didn't read it," protested Hiro. "Let me have it tonight and I'll return it to you tomorrow."

"No, Hiro. I've got to have it tonight. Tack wants to see it. Come on over sometime and I'll show it to you."

"Okay."

They walked off in the opposite direction. Over his shoulders, Hiro watched his brother disappear into the dark. "I hope against hope for Frank."

"It's no use, Hiro. He's a diehard."

"I'm going to keep trying," he said doggedly.

13

"Let's pay a social call," said Tad to Hiro after supper.

"Where?" he asked, helping his mother gather the used dishes and bowls into the dishpan.

There was a twinkle in Tad's eyes as he glanced quickly at his friend. They were inseparable now. They could be comfortable with one another in silence. They would talk only if necessary.

"To Tack's place," Tad said brightly. He carefully brushed back his hair. "We can gain much by visiting them. There'll be Frank, of course, and others whom we ought to know and watch."

"All right," he said. Then he knitted his brows. "Maybe we're not welcome. Suppose they kick us out?"

Tad chuckled lightly. "All the better for our knowledge. We'll know where we stand with the opposition."

"Nothing like trying. And I want to see Frank again. He's getting too popular and powerful for comfort."

"You can't suppress him, Hiro. He's beyond us. He's got something which we lack."

"Who says we can't stop him? Hell, I must. He's bitching our family name. Last night I couldn't sleep worrying about it."

"How? How will you do it?" Tad shrugged his shoulders. "Come on, Hiro. Let's get going."

They walked down the road in the growing dusk. A lone sea gull flapped its wings sharply overhead, hurrying before sundown.

"Yes, he's got something. Some brother—yours," Tad said.

"Today he won over three more boys. And what are we doing about it? Nothing!"

"Why not learn his sales talk while we're visiting tonight? Maybe we can do the same trick for our group."

"Lay off the kidding, Tad. We must act and quick."

Tack Saiki's apartment was lit bright and cheery. Both Frank and Tack Saiki were home, and they had company. "General" Mita and his son Harry were visiting, and also John Tabe.

Frank pulled out a couple of benches for Hiro and Tad. He showed no curiosity nor resentment of their visit.

"Well, I'll run along," John Tabe said, his voice chilling as words left his mouth.

"What's your hurry, John?" Tack Saiki said. "You just came."

"Yes, I must go. I'll be back." The door closed behind John Tabe.

"He doesn't like us, Hiro," Tad told him with a smile.

Tack Saiki rose and switched on the lights. Going to the windows, he pulled down the shades.

"Well, what's on your mind?" Frank said genially to them.

"We came to pay a social call," Tad said, smiling. He glanced about the group, looking in particular at the Issei, "General" Mita. "Are we in the way?"

"No, you're not," said Frank easily. "Join our discussion. The General here was discussing on the Asia-for-Asiatics theme."

"It's been a long time," the General said, glancing at Hiro interestedly.

"Yes, since Tanforan," Hiro acknowledged, studying the Issei. His figure had grown paunchy. Now his face was well fed and contented. He remembered the day when the old man was christened the "General" in Tanforan. He was the easy-chair strategist who talked nothing but war to everybody. "How is the war progressing, General?" he asked, smiling.

The General nodded approvingly. "Japan will win. Her spirit will carry her to glory and triumph."

"Still the same General Mita," Hiro said, watching the old man's proud face. You were once a janitor in San Francisco. You were once humble and weak... a has-been, he thought coldly. Then he pitied him. Now you take pride in Japan's initial success. That gives you a lift, doesn't it? It makes you great and big, as if you accomplished something yourself, as if, after all, your life was not in vain. It makes you feel like a new man.

"You boys volunteered for the United States Army?" the General said, looking sharply at Hiro and Tad. "Well! So you did. So you did. It's a lost cause, boys. Japan is your country. She claims you but not America. She does not want you. Frank, here, is wise. He chooses Japan."

"You're mistaken, General. My country is America but I am not fighting for any nation," Frank said. "I fight for man and his rights."

"Better that you belong to the winning side, boys," the General said, nonplused. "In Asia you will be equal. There you will have a future. Orientals have no chance in America. See what they did with us Japanese! Just because we're of the yellow race they evacuated us. See how they allowed German and Italian aliens to remain in their homes! We are not equals here."

Harry, the General's son, cut in eagerly. "You guys ought to think it over. There's still time before the induction."

"Time for what?" Hiro said shortly.

"Time for you guys to buck the draft."

Tad laughed outright. "This is rich! Did you hear that, Hiro?"

"Why should we fight for America when our future is not here?" Harry demanded. "Why should we risk our necks? Look at the suckers who fought in the last war! What did they get? They're forgotten men."

"Harry, do you realize what you're getting into?" Tad asked, bristling, but his voice cool and deliberate.

This was a mistake. We should have never come, Hiro thought. Frank's too clever. He'll never open up now. We should leave right now but with no hard feelings. We bungled again.

Harry smiled, showing his perfect teeth. "Anything is better than a soldier's life. Let them put me in jail. I'll at least have my life when they let me loose after the war."

Hiro rose abruptly, and looking at Tad, he said, "We must be going. We have another place to go."

"Aw, stick around, fellows," Tack Saiki said, snickering.

When Tad got to his feet, Frank accompanied them to the door. "Drop around again, fellows," he said.

"Next time, come around prepared so you can stay a long time," Tack Saiki called, chuckling.

They walked down the road. Now darkness covered the camp. A few bulb lights of the block swayed in the north wind.

"We missed fire again. It was all wrong," Hiro said gloomily.

"We learned one thing over there—not to see them in a group," Tad said lightly. "Let's go see Yosh Yoshida. We never did talk seriously with him."

"It's no use, Tad. Yosh is all for Frank's ideas now."

"Come on. Are you giving up already? Where's your fight?" Tad cried, slapping him on the back. "If he's not alone, we'll just say hello and leave. Okay?"

"He lives in an unfriendly block," Hiro said skeptically. "They don't like us—those Tule-bound people."

"Are you coming? I'm going to see him and have a little talk," Tad said, walking off.

Hiro joined him in the dark alley. "I don't like it, Tad. Something gives me the creeps tonight."

"Don't be a wet blanket. Let's get that funny taste out of our mouths. We'll do better at Yosh's."

Hiro followed a few paces behind him as they came to the puddles. They walked single file up the road. Now they were passing the darkened mess hall. Pussywillows swayed in the wind, casting a shadow across their path. Then more shadows appeared to multiply and converge into a solid darkness. Just as Tad reached the intersection, Hiro saw the scuffle.

"Hiro, help!" Tad cried to him.

He rushed toward Tad and his assailants, his thoughts numb with the swiftness of the event. This is it. This is it.

Then he heard the footsteps behind him, and instinctively he turned his head. As a face bobbed up in front of him, he simultaneously closed his eyes and ducked. There was a dull ringing in his head, and he was aware of the blows that rained on his head, neck, and shoulders. The ground shook violently. He felt himself sinking lower and lower till he knew no more.

14

When his eyes opened he saw her. His head ached dully and he scarcely smiled. His eyes blinked in the bright sunlight. "Where am I?" he said.

"You're home, Hiro," Jean said, bending over him.

Yes, his mind said. There is your bookstand. On the shelf is your radio. There is your bedlamp, your homemade nightstand, your collection of arrowheads and rocks. This is my home. Yes, I am home. "How long have I been back?" he asked anxiously. "What's happened to Tad?"

"Hush. Don't ask questions now," she said. "Oh, darling. I'm so glad now."

Then he saw Tad hovering at the foot of the bed. His mother came scurrying with a bowl of chicken soup. He forced a smile. Yes, he was home. This was his complete world. Beyond the door a strange, hostile life lay waiting for him.

"Tad," he said. Tad came to his side, grinning abashedly.

"How are you, old man?" Tad said.

He tried to nod, and then he was conscious of his bandage on his head. He touched his head tenderly. Then he quizzically looked at his friend's face. There was a patch over his left brow. A shallow cut below the cheek still showed a trace of healing.

"What happened that night, Tad? How did I get home?"

"I brought you home." Tad smiled.

"What happened after I fell?"

"They chased me but I got away. I got several cuts and bruises, that's all. And when I came to where you lay, I got help. An Issei helped me carry you home."

Hiro wetted his lips slowly. "Who were they?"

"I don't know. They wore their hats low over the eyes."

"You could not tell?"

"No."

Jean interrupted them. "Rest now, Hiro. There will be time for talk. Rest now."

He closed his eyes. He felt her cool hand on his forehead. He opened his eyes and smiled at her and then closed them. Now I must rest. I am hurt, he told himself. When I get well I will become busy. Then there will be no rest.

He dozed fitfully. When he awoke his mother was hovering over him solicitously. He heard Jean and Tad talking at the table. "Yes, Jean. A couple more new fellows joined up with Frank. We're losing," Tad was saying.

"Oh, we must do something. Can't you report this to the authorities?" Jean was talking. "Oh, this is shameful. We must stop these threats and beatings. We must stop Frank."

"How?" Tad was asking helplessly.

"There must be a solution," she was crying. "This is intolerable."

The voices died down, and his mother faded away. Then he dozed straightway and awoke again. Night came, and the lights dazzled his eyes till Jean shaded the naked bulbs with Bristol board. Darkness came and with it the silence of the early hours. Dawn's light filtered into the room as his eyes opened again, rested and eager.

Now he saw his mother waking with the mess hall's breakfast call. And he heard the morning rush to work, the flurry of voices and the roar of traffic. Jean came running into the room, wearing a bright new apron, breathless and vibrant.

Oh, sweet, his heart called. I am well already. Worry not. Our day will come before long. Sing, Jean. Laugh, Jean. Life is now.

She came over, skipping lightly. "Feeling better, darling?" She patted his cheek and in the same swift moment she put on the coffee percolator. Watching his shining eyes, she dialed his favorite program of waltz music.

Humming "Blue Danube," she brought him a pan of warm water and his toothbrush and paste. She waltzed gracefully from there and yon, watching his sparkling eyes all the while.

You are my song. You are the heart of my life, he sang. You are my salve in pain; you bring solace in sadness; you take away defeats and return with laughter.

Now his mother returned with the food, and Jean helped her at the stove.

"Oh, haven't you eaten yet, Mama?" Jean said, noticing the two servings.

"No," his mother said. "I do not wish to eat at the mess hall anymore."

Hiro did not turn to see her but his mind churned her words. I know, I know, he thought. She does not say so but her world is getting narrower and narrower. She does not say but I know. Her world is wide and boundless. Cringe not, Mama. The spell shall be broken. I will do the job for what is right.

And then the waltz music rushed into his ears again.

One afternoon he was back on his feet. He walked with a limp that slowed him considerably and only ventured to the front steps.

"You should not walk yet," Jean scolded him, watching him limp painfully.

"I need fresh air and sunlight." He looked irritated and restless. "I'm getting sick and tired lolling around here. I should be on the move."

"You must be completely healed before you get busy," she warned him. "There's no use in hurrying unless you can do a thorough job."

"I am ready," he said quickly.

"You may be ready but you mess it up each time." Her honesty grated him. "Accomplishments—that's what counts. Without accomplishments what good are readiness and words?"

"Don't be impatient, Jean."

"I'm not impatient." Her eyes darted fire suddenly.

"I'm doing my best," he said, defending himself. "I'm planning all the while."

"What are you going to do about that beating you got?" she asked furiously. "You don't know who they were? What can you plan?"

His face reddened. His hands trembled. On his lips was the retort that would sting. Here is the beginning of our first quarrel, he thought. This is a pretty setup.

"What are you going to do about your brother?" she insisted doggedly.

"I don't see how you can sit still and watch him toy with you like a baby."

A minute ago you told me to take it easy, he thought grimly. Now you are impatient for action.

"Frank is making life miserable for me. Everybody knows what he's doing," she said grievously. "And my friends ask me if I approve Frank's choice."

"I'll take care of Frank."

"You must do something about him. I cannot remain with you unless you stop him."

"No, Jean!"

"Yes, I mean it." Her voice was firm and final. "I won't stay. I can't stay."

"Listen, Jean. Please."

"Not when I think of my brother Jack and what I sacrificed for you."

Lord, oh lord, he thought. It is coming. The day is coming. Easy there, boy. Now is no time for words. Think it over; make no rash talk. Take a cut; swing freely; go all the way. Let it ride now but remember. "Let me handle Frank," he said softly. "You don't need to worry, sweet."

Now she looked tired and ill, her temper spent. She stood tiny and frail beside him, fingering his coat sleeve. I have been cruel and beastly, he thought. I have forgotten her worries. Her parents in Tule Lake and Jack with the 442nd Infantry. And now she is taking over my family's headache.

He gently put his arm around her waist, and the couple stood silently together watching the sun streaks hit the barrack across the way. And slowly color returned to her face and her eyes became now alive and then soft as they sought his tender and troubled ones.

15

You are not alone, he told himself. You have many counterparts behind you. You act separately and yet it all ties in. You have faces with distinct differences; you see many colors in men and nature; you are working for your own goals and ideals. You see life as you see; you react uniquely. Your actions are the beginnings of a new form. But you are not alone. You and another you and another you make colors and variations. You are of one cloth; you are of one family; you are of one world. You and you must learn to live together. What you do will affect another. What you say will concern another. What another says or does will involve you.

"I came to see how you were getting along. Any better?" Frank asked anxiously.

"I'm all right," he said, not without conviction. "And you, Frank?"

"As usual," he said cheerfully. "Hear the latest about me?"

"No. What is it?"

"I got an induction paper from the local board."

"You haven't gone for your physical examination yet," Hiro exclaimed incredulously.

Frank smiled slowly. "My penalty for writing that letter of protest. I expected it."

"What are you going to do?"

"Refuse—of course."

"The FBI will get you," he cried unhappily. "You don't want them to pick you up, do you?"

"I'm ready for any consequence."

"Frank, do you know what you're doing?"

"Yes. Perfectly."

Hiro waved his hand in a frantic gesture. "Remember Papa."

"I remember his sayings, Hiro," Frank said softly. He placed his hand on Hiro's shoulder. "Did he not say this: 'Man must fight for what is right to reach harmony, and God made us so each one of us has a spark capable of giving light to others.'"

"You remember, yes. Are you following them?"

"Yes, I'm working for harmony just as much as you are. You said this war is a process for the coming harmony and that we are participants, did you not?"

"Yes. And you said by refusing to participate you are working for harmony!"

"I did," Frank said, nodding in assent. "Did he not say, 'Harmony results from clashes of ideas'? It is a process with trials and errors. I may make mistakes on the way but fundamentally I shall be on the right road."

"Remember what Papa said about willingness?" he asked in turn. "He said that it is the will to harmonize more than anything else which will save the people's world. That is what he told us, remember?"

"Yes." Frank rose to his feet and stretched his arms. "And where does this get us? We agree here and then disagree in action. Why can we not get together? We're both fighting for harmony."

"Yes. I will fight on the battlefield and you behind the front." Hiro looked squarely in his eyes. Then his eyes softened. "You will not change your course?"

Frank slowly shook his head. The air was charged with silence and expectance. No use, bub, Hiro thought dully. How can I change him? As Papa said, 'Harmony must come from within in order to embrace without.' I am helpless. I should talk. I have not yet committed myself to fight. I must prove myself before harmony will become my work.

Then he recalled his father's familiar words that always struck him between the eyes: 'Harmony is man's stepchild—he must give more for less return and find solace in the child's growth.' Yes, he must give himself to the cause. Now it was make or break for him just as it would be on the battlefield later. He must pitch in; he must take a cut. Cleanly. Yes, he was ready. Yes, he was in.

"Guess I'll mosey along," Frank said as he walked toward the door. He hesitated at the last moment. "Maybe this will be the last time we'll be together."

"When is your induction date?"

"The fifteenth—in ten days."

"Time is short."

"Don't expect to see me hereafter," Frank said. "I may be picked up at any hour."

"How shall I explain this to Mama?" Hiro asked, his voice just above a whisper.

"Tell her fully after I'm taken away but not before." Frank opened the door and walked out.

"Frank," he called quickly. He walked with a slight limp to the door.

"What's the matter?" asked Frank, returning with a slight frown on his face.

"I've been thinking of this right along but never told you. How about going up to Salt Lake with me and spend the weekend there?" Hiro asked eagerly. "It'll be the last time together for a long while. And maybe the fresh air will do us good."

Frank smiled. "Sounds good after two years in camp. It would be my last fling, I'm sure."

"What do you say? I can get the short-term leave for us right away. We can make it this weekend."

"Are you trying to convert me at the last minute? No soap if you are," Frank said suspiciously.

"No. I've given up, Frank," he said. "It'll be our last time together."

"All right. I'll go if you can arrange it."

"Great!" he cried eagerly. "We'll do the town red, Frank. You haven't been there but I have, and let me tell you—the city reminds you of San Francisco. It gives you that back home feeling. The city lights and traffic awaken you. It's a tonic, Frank."

"I guess so."

"Then there's the most beautiful view of the city from the Alta Building. There you can almost believe you're in San Francisco again. The foggy mist over the city reminds you of the bay, and the lake looks like an ocean."

"Ah, San Francisco," Frank said. He added eagerly. "Where's this building? Be sure to take me there."

"You bet. It's a beauty of a building too—a ten-story skyscraper. Reminds you of home."

Frank impulsively grabbed him by the shoulders and said warmly, "Thanks, old man."

16

Hiro stood nervously smoking by the window. With continuous jerky movements he looked at the skyline. Cigarette butts lay strewn on the floor. He glanced at his watch. Crushing his cigarette, he lit another in a moment. Ten stories below he could see people streaming on the street like ants. Noiselessly he opened the window, and a rush of cool air entered the hall.

The rolling door of the elevator echoed through the corridor. He cocked his head and listened for the familiar footsteps. A stranger walked past the wing and entered an office in the adjoining passageway.

He's late, he thought. Isn't he coming? He looked at the time. He flipped his half-smoked cigarette to the floor. The elevator stopped again. A sound of quick footsteps came down the hall. Then he saw him.

"Sorry, old man," Frank said, breathless and excited as he rushed forward to greet him. "I bumped into a pal of mine and we had a drink together."

"That's okay." He indicated the skyline. "How'd you like that?"

"Whew!" Frank took his hat off, whistling as he approached closer to the window. "Boy, this is something."

"See the Great Salt Lake, Frank?" he said, pointing to the lake. "Doesn't that mist look like San Francisco fog?"

"Jesus Christ." He whistled softly. "This is like homecoming. San Francisco—that's the place. I hope we can go back there as free citizens and return to what we've been used to."

"We will eventually," he said, looking at the windowsill fixedly.

Frank edged closer to the open window, peering toward north.

"See that hill and those buildings up there?" Hiro said, leaning forward together with Frank. "That's where I went on my last trip."

"What is it?"

"Fort Douglas."

Frank nodded silently.

Hiro stepped back a moment. He measured the angle of his brother's body and the window. Frank glanced back, and pointing to the statuesque building he asked, "Isn't that the Hotel Utah?"

"That's right," Hiro agreed. He paused before joining Frank. "Have a good time?" he asked.

"Much, very much. Fancy shops, parks, shows, cafes, bars—who can ask for more?"

"Frank, do you still feel the same way about your induction?" Hiro said, barely audible to Frank.

"Yes," answered Frank slowly. "I won't change, Hiro." Hiro stood quietly beside his brother. Frank straightened excitedly. Several times he beat his chest vigorously as he inhaled the cool, clean air. Then he poked his head out of the window, crying, "Great! This is great!"

"I'll say. When I came up here the last time I felt like a new man," he said, backing away a trifle.

He straightened quickly. Frank remained stationary, his head out of the window. Hiro's outstretched hands trembled. He reached forward with his hands out and flat like a gardener's hoe. Frank straightened up and looked back at him.

Hiro's wan face broke into a smile. He intimately grasped his brother's shoulders. As he noted Frank's dying interest in the skyline view, his eyes turned cold.

His face hardened but his voice became soft and nervous. "Look at that beauty walking up the street. See? Over there."

"Where?" Frank leaned forward once more, his head jutting out of the window.

"There! See?"

He stepped behind Frank. In one swift, surging moment Hiro charged forward and pushed him out the window. Down below, screams and shouts froze the air. A police whistle blew shrilly. Far away a siren began screaming.

Leaning heavily against the wall, he violently shook his head. His legs, bent and trembling, buckled under him. He sat there, his eyes unseeing and staring, his mind racing with thoughts. Take a cut. Follow through. Go all the way.

Then slowly and deliberately, he rose to his feet. As he walked toward the elevator and before pressing the button for "down," he pushed back his hair and straightened his tie.

—c. 1944

Unfinished Message

Unfinished Message

It was on a chilly May night in 1945 in the middle of Utah desert when my mother sharply called me. "I can't sleep tonight," she said. True, she had been fretting the past few nights, and I knew she was worried over her son at the Italian front.

I reassured her that everything would be all right. Hadn't he, I reasoned with her, come through without a scratch with a full year's service at the front, even with the 442nd Infantry Regiment?

"But I keep seeing Kazuo's face tonight," she said. "Each time I'm about to fall asleep his face keeps coming back."

I tried to calm her fears as best as I could. Nevertheless, she did not sleep that night.

The next night and the night following she slept fitfully more or less. Beneath her outward calm, however, she was under an ordeal only a mother could understand. "No news is good news. He's all right," I assured her.

A few days later we received a wire from the War Department that Kazuo had been seriously wounded. The news almost killed her. In the full medical report following we learned that he had a fractured skull but was resting peacefully. What struck me as odd was the day my brother was wounded. It was on May 5, the very night my mother was unable to sleep.

When we received word again, it was more cheerful. Kazuo was coming back on the hospital ship destined for home, and we were to decide the hospital nearest our home. We were still living in Topaz, Utah Relocation Center at the time, and the nearest available Army hospital was the Fitzsimmons in Colorado.

"Let's have him transferred there so we can visit him as soon as he comes home," I said to Mother.

My mother would have none of it. "Do you think this is our real home? Our home is back in San Leandro, California. We'll be moving from here again, and Kazuo too will have to transfer. No, we'll go back and Kazuo can go to a hospital in California."

My mother couldn't get out of the camp soon enough. She counted the days when the next train to California would take us back home. In the meantime we learned that Kazuo was being transferred to DeWitt Army Hospital in Auburn, California.

On our trip home, our train stopped for a few minutes at Auburn, and our first urge was to get off the train and visit Kazuo. My mother stared toward the Auburn interiors. "It must be only a few miles from here. Here we are, so close to him and yet so far."

We heeded our good judgment and did not get off the train. "We must make ready our home. It must be in a mess. We must first go home and get busy cleaning the place. Our home must resemble our old home for Kazuo."

It took us two weeks to clean the house and settle down. My mother had to apply to the United States Attorney's office for a travel permit because she was an enemy alien and Japan and the United States were still at war. Secure with a permit my mother accompanied me to Auburn. All the way on the bus to the hospital she nervously weighed the seriousness of Kazuo's actual condition. Are his legs all intact, are his hands there? she wondered. Can he see, is he normal mentally? Not until she saw him in person did she feel relieved. He could see, his hands were usable, but his legs? Mother talked constantly of everything she could think of but his condition. Before long, she became aware of his actual condition.

In order to relieve ourselves of the hot valley air caught inside of the ward, my brother suggested sitting on the screened porch. It was when the ward boy saw my brother moving on the bed that he came to help him to his wheelchair. The ward boy bodily lifted him on the chair, and Mother saw my brother's spindly legs. He was unable to walk.

Afterwards, Mother asked me to inquire of the doctor about Kazuo's condition. Will he ever walk? The doctor I talked to was not too hopeful, but I did not tell Mother.

"He says there's a fifty-fifty possibility that Kazuo will walk," I said to Mother.

Coming home, Mother said, "I'm worried over him. If I only could live long enough to see him fully recovered."

After another operation on his head, my brother was transferred to Letterman Hospital in San Francisco, making possible weekly visits for Mother and I. Each time we saw him, she would take me aside and ask, "Do you think he's much improved? Isn't he better?"

That Christmas my brother got a two-week furlough and came home for the first time since the war had started. I had to help him with his bath and toilet. My brother was confined to his wheelchair.

Time and again, Mother would ask me, "Will he ever walk again? I can't tell him that I worry over him."

Before my brother was released from the hospital, Mother died in her sleep on August 5, 1946. Although she complained of pains in the neck, we were totally unprepared for her death. Her doctor had previously diagnosed her symptoms as arthritis, but her death was sudden.

After her death our house became dark and silent. Even when my brother returned home for good in a wheelchair, the atmosphere was unchanged. We seemed to be companions in the dark. However, it changed one day.

As I sat quietly in the living room I heard a slight tapping on the window just above the divan where my mother had slept her last. When the taps repeated again, I went outside to check, knowing well that a stiff wind could move a branch of our lemon tree with a lemon or two tapping the wall of our house. There was no wind, no lemon near enough to reach the window. I was puzzled but did not confide in my brother when he joined me in the living room.

I had all but forgotten the incident when my brother and I were quietly sitting in the living room near the spot where our mother had passed away. For a while I was not conscious of the slight tapping on the window. When the repeated taps were loud enough to be heard clearly, I first looked at the window and then glanced at my brother. He too had heard the taps.

"Did you hear that?" I said.

My brother nodded. "Sure," he said. "Did you hear it too? I heard it the other day but I thought it was strange."

We looked at the window. There were no birds in sight, no lemons tapping. Then the taps repeated. After a few moments of silence I was about to comment when we heard the tapping again. This time I looked silently at my brother and on tiptoes approached the window. The tapping continued so I softly touched the windowpane. The instant my fingers touched the glass, it stopped.

My brother and I looked at each other, silently aware that it must have been Mother calling our attention. At that instant I became conscious of the purpose of the mysterious taps. I couldn't help but recall Mother's words, "I can't stop worrying over you, my son."

The tapping stopped once and for all after that. We never heard it again after the message had reached us.

—1947

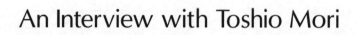

An Interview with Toshio Mori

Toshio Mori celebrating the publication of Woman from Hiroshima *at the Oakland Museum, January 1980. Photo by Steven Mori. All photos in this section are
from the collection of Steven Mori.*

An Interview with Toshio Mori

"Everyday immortality," Toshio Mori's own way of describing a person in one of his short stories, also distinguished the life and work of Toshio Mori. For over fifty years, Toshio Mori through his stories and novels has given meaning and immortality to the daily aspirations, struggles, and joys of ordinary people—the Japanese American gardeners, house-wives, workers, artists, and students who were his friends and neighbors.

Through the power and compassion of his words, Toshio Mori will continue to show us how to "grab the grits of life, scraping for crumbs while cooking up the great feast of life."

Toshio Mori is a pioneer Japanese American writer living in San Leandro, California. His second book of short stories is *The Chauvinist and Other Stories* (Asian American Studies Center, UCLA, 1979). *Yokohama, California*, Mori's first short-story collection, was published in 1949.

The interviewer wishes to thank Michael Butler for his assistance and taping of the interview, and Jean Yip for her transcription. The interview took place in San Leandro, California, 9 October 1979, and is edited for publication. Note: An earlier interview of Toshio Mori by Peter Horikoshi can be found in *Counterpoint: Perspectives on Asian America* (Asian American Studies Center, UCLA, 1976).

Toshio Mori died 12 April 1980, as this issue of *Amerasia Journal* was going to press. Our staff hopes that the issue, focusing on the language

---

Reprinted with permission from *Amerasia Journal*.

*Mori was the third of four sons born to Yoshi and Hidekichi
Mori. Photo circa 1911 by Komai Arai.*

and literature of Asian America and including a recent interview with Mori, will help to celebrate the rich vision of life Toshio Mori has given us.

—*Russell Leong*

> ... what emerged for me was the panorama of Japanese America in the early 1930s, in the later thirties as the storm clouds gathered, and in the concentration camps of 1942– 45, stretched on a canvas from here to there, a veritable Floating World. No one else has kept this account of our lives, in fiction and in personal essay, in such detail, with such compassion.
>
> —Hisaye Yamamoto, from the introduction to *The Chauvinist and Other Stories* by Toshio Mori

Leong: Toshio, thank you for inviting us into your home. It's difficult to know where to begin, as your writing career spans half a century. The majority of your hundreds of short stories are about the first and second generations of Japanese Americans in the Oakland–San Leandro East Bay region of Northern California. Yet they represent more than the stories of several generations. They capture the essence of Japanese American community life in the crucial decades before, during, and after the Second World War.

Let's begin with your earliest memories as a child.

Family and the Daily Work

Mori: The earliest childhood memories that I recall are between the ages of two through five. I was born in Oakland, 1910, so I remember quite distinctly early Oakland, especially around Seventh, Eighth, and Ninth Streets, which was at that time more or less the central part, so-called downtown Oakland.

I recall the pungent smells of a bakery shop near the corner of Washington and Seventh Streets. The smell of fresh bread used to always fascinate me. Also, I remember the Chinese laundry across the street from my father's bathhouse where I was born. I used to see the Chinese laundrymen stand on the top of the flat roof where they had outdoor clotheslines.

Leong: Can you tell us something about your father's bathhouse?

Toshio and his mother, Yoshi, circa 1913–1914.

Mori: The bathhouse used to fascinate me because I was born there on the mezzanine floor, which was just a stair that my father had built in the rear—so-called living quarters—of the bathhouse. As older people might recall, in the old days, a bathhouse was a flourishing business because most people seldom had bathroom facilities.

Leong: Did your whole family help in the bathhouse?

Mori: My two older brothers were still in Japan. At two years old, I was the only child living with my parents. I didn't help very much during that young period. The only memory that I have was that I used to play with a bat and ball up and down the bathhouse hall. I believe that's when I started to feel sportwise, and I always preferred baseball to other sports. After my mother came from Japan, she took charge of the bathhouse business. My father was always black with soot because he had to fire the coal stove, furnace, fire up, heat the water. It was very seldom that my father ever went up front because he was always dirty with coal and wood.

Leong: So, actually, running a bathhouse was a twenty-four-hour job....

Mori: Well, I believe it must have been about late evening, probably about eight or nine o'clock, that business closed. My father had the bathhouse till about the end of 1913, and then from there he went into partnership with our two relatives, and formed a florist and a nursery. He sold his bathhouse and we moved to Sixteenth Street, near that Southern Pacific depot in Oakland. The nursery site, at that time, is the present Oakland post office building. There I spent about two years until about 1915 and attended kindergarten.

I moved to San Leandro in summer of 1915. At that time, the present [place] where I live was more or less country area and we used to think we were traveling far when we did visit San Leandro. San Leandro was known for cherry trees, so it was called the "cherry city" but it also had a few sprinklings of Japanese nurseries. Of course, the white Americans owned nurseries too.

The Japanese principally raised carnations and roses, but we also raised outdoor flowers. My father started mostly with the outdoor plants such as dahlias, chrysanthemums, daffodils, for all the seasonal outdoor cut-flower business. We had greenhouses, so we raised cyclamen plants, plus freesias.

Leong: What was the daily work in the nursery like in those days?

Mori: I believe I helped some, but as a child, since my parents were

Family portrait at the San Leandro nursery, circa 1914. Top row: Mr. Naito (Mori family relative and nursery co-owner) and Masao (Toshio's older brother). Second row: Tadashi (Toshio's second-oldest brother), Yoshi (mother), and Hidekichi (father). Front row: Kazuo (Toshio's younger brother), and Toshio.

very busy, I was on my own, and they gave me the freedom to do as I wished with my free period. Since I was probably the only Asian child in the neighborhood at that time, I was more or less a novelty even among the neighborhood children. At first I was not accepted but later, as I started to associate, I became one of the boys of the group in my neighborhood.

Leong: What did your father and mother do in the nursery?

Mori: My father was a very hard-working man and he used to work probably sixteen hours at least during the day because he would wake up early in the morning. Between six-thirty and seven he would be at work and remain working, with the exception of lunch and supper time, till late in the evening. And my mother also accompanied him as much as possible with just cooking added. She would help cut and bunch the flowers and also remained with the nursery work until late evening. So, as a child, I had to find my own way to occupy myself and that's the reason why I was able to do my own thing.

My mother said I had to be responsible for whatever I did, so from early age I had to account for myself and I had to more or less take care of myself. Whatever I did, bad or good, it would be my responsibility. So, in a way, that helped me when I started to commute to Oakland— which is about twelve miles from San Leandro. From second grade on I had my public education in Oakland plus studying at the Japanese language school in the afternoon after American school. I was very much away from the influence of my parents during the school age.

As I mentioned, my mother told me to be on my own, so I was able to do anything. I did associate with some rough elements during my boyhood days but I never did get into trouble myself. But I knew the rough life too because one of my near relatives was a chauffeur for a gambling house in Oakland Chinatown. Whenever I used to travel by there he would give me money, coins, from twenty-five cents, ten cents, sometimes fifty cents even, because when his customers on the limousine would tip him big, in turn, he would give me tips and say "treat yourself." So I used to go by there every day. Very seldom would he not give me anything, as usually he used to have winners, since he carried them from morning to night. He was very nice to me so I also used to get ideas because he would tell me the customers' lives.

Top: Toshio playing with younger brother Kazuo, circa
1918. Bottom: In his teenage years, Mori played shortstop with the Oakland Merritts. Toshio and fellow
player Oishi, circa 1926.

Leong: What did you do as a teenager?

Mori: I helped at the nursery during the summertime and I also helped at my brother's store. From the age of nine, I used to help clean the flowers. Probably I helped more in my brother's shop because I spent most of my daily hours in Oakland, so whenever I had some extra time, I helped my brother polish the mirrors in the shop, mop the floors, clean the buckets, flower vases.

Leong: I understand that in your early twenties, you worked in the nurseries from twelve to sixteen hours a day, but you also made up your mind to be a writer. Before you made this decision, you had also wanted to become an artist, a Buddhist missionary, and a major-league baseball player. Could you tell us what clinched your decision to become a writer?

Mori: At first, when I was in grade school, I had interest more or less in art—drawings. I was pretty good at it, I guess, as far as childhood drawings were concerned, which led me to read some of the books. And from that I started to read some of the dime novels, which were popular at that period. For ten cents you were able to read these paper edition books. The titles were by Frank Merriwell, that's baseball stories.... And then there were Nick Carter detective stories and Horatio Alger stories, which were more or less about a poor boy becoming rich or famous. We used to trade the dime novels for a nickel to get a second copy. By returning the copy we used to pay only a nickel, so I was able to read many of these dime novels. That interest started to draw me toward literature at a low level.

From there I always did have a hankering for writing. English at that time was quite difficult for any Asian Americans because our parents spoke very little English. At home we used to speak our own language; for me it was Japanese. My parents were fluent in Japanese but not at all in English and so all the English I learned was at school, nowhere else.

During the teenage years, I started to get more interested in writing because I had an English teacher in high school who more or less had influence on me. Her interest was in composition and I happened to write one that was fairly well done. She gave me encouragement, and for four years, I took various English courses from her.

From dime novels I started to take interest in short stories. Through old magazines and also books I started to take interest in O. Henry,

Stephen Crane; the French writers, de Maupassant, Balzac; and also Katherine Mansfield stories; and then the short stories of Chekhov, Gorki, Golgol, and almost all the Russian writers. I took interest in short stories at the beginning, and from there I returned back to the United States and became interested in Sherwood Anderson. His stories used to puzzle me at the beginning and that made me want to write and also to read into Sherwood Anderson. In fact, I believe I've read everything of Sherwood Anderson's to understand him. My first interest became his *Winesburg Ohio*. One day I started to feel akin to his characters and at the same time I started to find that I, through the combination of characters I knew in the Japanese community, became more fluent in characterizing the typical Japanese people within my community.

Early Writings

Leong: Do you remember your first story?

Mori: I just remember vaguely; it was about my older Hawaiian friend. He was a Nisei Hawaiian who came to America to study engineering. I was sort of attached to him, because at that time he was manager of the Nisei baseball club, and so he not only encouraged me in playing ball with the older boys, but also took some interest in me personally.

Leong: What were your first writings about?

Mori: I believe the first stories were mostly autobiographical narratives. From there I started to head towards commercialism, thinking of gaining more money, and so I started to study some of the commercial type of stories such as in the *Saturday Evening Post* or *Collier's* or *Liberty*. For a while I started to get pretty close to, I believe, acceptance, but that too became my side interest because my personal experiences started to become more dominant in my interest. My nearest subjects were Japanese communities because that's where I resided, where I played and experienced, and also worked. So my concentration started to bend towards the Japanese, so-called Japanese life-relations. As I became more adept in writing, I believe I concentrated more in Japanese American relations.

Leong: As your stories took on more Japanese American themes, did you write for the Japanese Americans to read or for the outside general audience?

Budding carnations in the family greenhouses. This photograph was one in a series of professional photos taken for the purpose of publicizing the release of Yokohama, California, *circa 1948–1949. Photo by R. B. Laing.*

Wedding portrait of Toshio and Hisayo Yoshiwara, June 29, 1947. Photo by Shigetomi Studio, Oakland.

Top: Toshio, son Steven, and Hisayo at a family wedding, circa 1958. Bottom: Toshio and Hisayo, at the Woman from Hiroshima book party, January 1980. Photo by Robert Hsiang.

Mori: I was really trying my best to reach the white American readers in general, because I found that most of the writings by white Americans were concentrated on Japanese subjects through humor. Typical were stories by Peter B. Kyne, who wrote humorous Japanese angles, and most of them were based on detective, suspense, or mystery stories with the main character a Japanese detective. But as far as I was concerned, they didn't typify the Japanese community at all, and I started thinking that perhaps I could reveal some of the true Japanese lives by interpreting some of the characters I knew during that period.

Leong: In the beginning, though, you didn't submit your stories to English language sections of Japanese papers as other Nisei writers did. Is this because, as you said, you wanted a wider reading audience?

Mori: Yes. I believe I wanted to become a published writer and probably the only way I felt that I could become a published writer was through sales by regular American magazines. That was my first goal, to be published as a professional, and it took me six years before I was able to be accepted by a white magazine.... The first one, I believe, was "Tomorrow and Today." And the second one, which was taken at the same time, was "The Brothers." Those two stories are included in the *Yokohama* book.

Leong: You had mentioned that you had received enough rejection slips to paper a room. What do you think kept you going?

Mori: I wonder myself too, because there was so much discouragement that the first few rejections hit me hard. But when I started to receive so many rejections a day, then it became just automatic reflex, and it didn't hurt me that much. Rejections didn't mean much to me after that.

Leong: What type of reasons did the rejection letters give?

Mori: Well, the first few years when I was rejected I have to admit the writing was still slight stories, like sketches more than story, or simple narrative without probably a conclusion or a distinct effect on the readers. So I believe it was justified rejections because I still wasn't good enough to be understood by the readers.

Since my language was based on schooling in an American school and not at home as Sansei or Yonsei or Chinese who must be the fifth or sixth generation, I was handicapped with English. When I used to ride on a car I would study the English abridged dictionary and study the words. My first abridged dictionary had forty thousand words. I used to memorize all the words and for a while used to think I could write stories by basing them on a dictionary because that's where I studied the language. My language was awkward, and, as a whole, I believe I was a typical Nisei without high education. I probably used the language that was available at that time, more or less the spoken language. I think I tried to write my stories based on the spoken language because that typified my speaking language.

I also believe the white editors who were in charge of the magazines then felt that there was very little interest in anything Asian American because the population of the Asian Americans was almost nil in comparison to the national population; the only place where they were concentrated was in the state of California. But as I continued writing I did receive some encouraging letters back with the rejections, from various editors ranging from the little magazines to popular magazines such as *Collier's*, *Saturday Evening Post*, *Esquire*.

Leong: Can you tell us something about the Japanese American publications in the thirties and forties such as *Current Life* and *Nisei View*?

Mori: There used to be off and on attempts by the Nisei to publish Nisei stories and poems of that period, and there were amazingly quite a few Nisei poets and writers who did contribute to Japanese American newspapers in general. These Nisei, as a group, sometimes used to publish publications and one of them was *Current Life*. *Current Life* was probably the last publication before World War II and I happened to contribute to them because the editors wished that I submit some writings. *Current Life* was actually the individual effort of a Nisei couple who lived in San Francisco, James Omura and his wife, who happened to like publications. They published that on the side but they were hoping to make it into a self-sufficient Nisei publication. But Pearl Harbor Day came and disrupted their destiny.

Yokohama, California (1949)

Leong: It was a major achievement to publish your first collection of stories, *Yokohama, California*, right after the Second World War. The white critics such as William Saroyan and Lewis Gannett made their views at the time known through reviews. But what was the response of the Japanese American community to the book when it first came out?

Mori: As far as the white readers or white critics, they all gave me encouraging reviews, recognizing for the first time that there was Japanese American life existing in America. Until that time, as the older Californians remember, the Japanese living in California were much discriminated. When my book came out, they felt as if it was an introduction to the Japanese. It was the first book of stories of the Japanese American community and so it was quite well received. Probably the only negative criticism came from one of the Nisei critics in Southern California. And the book, as far as the Japanese Americans were concerned, the interest was generally good, but I don't believe there was enough interest to make a good sale. So my book didn't sell that much at the beginning.

The Chauvinist and Other Stories (1979)

Leong: The present UCLA collection, The Chauvinist, excludes all the stories in the Yokohama, California volume. Does it include any of the stories that the editors did not include in Yokohama?

Mori: Yes, I notice in The Chauvinist several that did not fit into Yokohama, California. Especially the story I remember distinctly was "Four-Bits." At that time, anything in sex was unacceptable in general reading, especially where some of the off-color situations arose.

Leong: "The Chauvinist," which is the lead story in this new collection, is an interesting title because the story is not about a male chauvinist at all. Can you tell us something about the story?

Mori: I believe that "The Chauvinist" was written in 1935. I wrote that as an experimental story, and I believe it was quite different at that time. I happened to bring it out a few years ago when Amerasia Journal sponsored the story contest. My first audience was my son, Steve, and I asked his opinion whether younger people would be interested in this story, retitled "The Chauvinist." He said: "Yeah, why don't you try it, submit it and see." And so it happened to win one of the three prizes. I know one of the teachers up in the Northwest asked me if I had just recently written it and I told him no, that I wrote that way back in the thirties. He was astounded because it fit the typical modern period.

Publicity photo of Toshio Mori with Yokohama, California, *circa 1949. Photo by Sus Niyeta.*

Publicity photo following the publication of Yokohama, California, *circa 1949. From left: Hidekichi (father), Hisayo (wife), Kazuo (youngest brother, wounded while serving in the 442nd Regimental Combat Team in WWII), and Toshio Mori. Photo by R. B. Laing.*

Leong: Who is the chauvinist?

Mori: Mainly it was based on a near relative of mine. This Issei was truly deaf and he had a very difficult time hearing his family's conversation. But whenever there was anything ill mentioned about him, his ears seemed to open up and he could hear very distinctly. Anything that was more or less objectionable to him would reach his ears. And so, this man who used to visit us became the main character in "The Chauvinist."

Leong: Many of your stories are about ordinary people, but they all have some extraordinary trait about them, such as this person who is deaf except when people say something bad about him, or as in the case of your mother, who can communicate without words.

Mori: Yes, I used to sit aside with these Issei friends of my parents' and listen quietly. I didn't take notes because probably they would object, so mentally I used to take down all their characteristics. I guess I got this trait from my mother, who was illiterate in English. She used to

Toshio's parents' house. Left to right: Mrs. Sara Kuniyoshi, Tadashi (brother), Toshio, Hisayo, Sada Mori (Masao's wife), Hidekichi (father), Kazuo (brother), Masao (brother), and Yasuo Kuniyoshi (an internationally known artist friend of Toshio's who was teaching at Mills College), circa 1949. Photo by R. B. Laing.

have extraordinary memory and could recite almost word for word, even the philosophical essays that I read to her. She would comment back to me in Japanese, and tell me things that I read and translated to her. And so I had a pretty good memory of each character, Issei character, who did come and spend the evening with my parents. For instance, this deaf [man] who came was actually despised by his family members because he had a mind of his own. Even if he had heard the instructions from his family members, he would do his own way. He would use his own technique, his own style, to do whatever they instructed him to do.

Leong: Toshio, can you describe some of the other people that made up your community, people that you wrote about?

Mori: Yes. I could mention some typical friends. Especially the Issei, the first generation Japanese. There was a Japanese laundryman who worked for a wealthy Piedmont family. He used to visit the local community churches especially since he was alone. He was very lonely and made friends with the local community. I used to listen to his discussions with other Issei and he gave me some of the characteristics of a Japanese who works for wealthy homes as a butler or laundryman. This Japanese was a laundryman but there were other Japanese who were so-called Japanese "schoolboys," butlers or cooks; all worked menial jobs within the house....

"1936"

Leong: In the story "1936," which was written in 1936, and which is in this new collection, you say that you want to know and experience everything. You were twenty-six years old at the time....

Mori: You see, 1936 was two years before my first story was accepted and published. The reason why I remember 1936 distinctly was because it was a period when I started concentrating on writing which began in 1932. So, in 1936, I was already writing to become a professional, for four years straight, including Sundays. And the writing habit that I scheduled for myself at the age of twenty-two in 1932 was for four hours daily including Sunday. My writing schedule was ten o'clock in the evening to two A.M. And I stuck with that schedule throughout my pre-war days. I believe I continued until the last evacuation day in 1942....

Zen

Leong: You do have a fascinating statement about a Zen priest, the one in "Hawaiian Note" in *The Chauvinist*. You said, "To me he was the humblest man I have ever met but I told him without hesitation, 'You are the most evil of men, more evil than anyone I know.'"

Mori: Yes, when our eyes met, he bowed before me when I first saw him at the door. His eyes told me that he was the most humble and when he bowed to me I couldn't get any below him. I was captured by his presence. Hisaye Yamamoto, who did the introduction, mentioned the Zen priest who read one of my stories, "The Trees" twenty-seven times. He not only read that story, he also re-read *Yokohama, California* about twenty-seven times to decipher the Zen angle. He says that it interested him so much that he re-read it twenty-seven times, and got different ideas.

The Zen technique is to enlighten each individual. To truly believe has to be an individual effort. When a Zen master is approached by a

Zen student, the master could immediately catch on whether that student has caught the Zen principle by saying "yes" or "no" or "black" and "white" or "I believe" or "I don't believe." If the student himself understands, he can match the master. He can not only follow but lead into the master's mind. And that's where the quality is for mutual understanding without words. Words, or language, is human effort where the human brain designs the invention of communication. But original communication was without language and emotions can be transmitted. When you reach that area you go into the Hinduism, or the part where the superman realm comes in.

I believe, in Zen, it's just one word would tell whether that man or the individual has the gift of understanding the Zen. When you say "yes," you should tell a Zen "yes" and you should know what a "yes" means. That's accepted as Zen. And if you say "no," that's also accepted as Zen. It's just a matter of understanding. For instance, in my story, what I believe is Zen is listed in that "Strange Bedfellows," where there are two students, one who acknowledges the presence of God, one who denies it. I believe, when I say "it," it should be understood the "it" means both ways.

Leong: Besides Asian religious works, are there any other Asian or Japanese writers or writings which have influenced you?

Mori: No, I had very little influence from the Japanese writers, even the famous, so-called past masters of Japan, so I had very little connection with Japanese literature as a background. Other than the Japanese local color in the study of the Japanese community here, I took very little reference into Japanese history or the past. Oddly, my interest in Asiatic books came from the study of New England literature. From Sherwood Anderson, I started to read back to the writing of the New England era—Walt Whitman, Ralph Waldo Emerson, and that group. When I started to read Whitman and Thoreau and Emerson, I found the Asiatic influence, especially the Japanese influence, so I started to look back into some of the Japanese or Asian books. Mainly the Indian books started to interest me. And at the same time, through philosophy, I became interested in religion and, for a while, when I was immersed in Indian books, my desire became towards priesthood and I was seriously thinking of going into religion as a minister.

Leong: Why didn't you?

Mori: Well, first of all, I wanted to be a monk who would stay up in a mountain retreat somewhat like Thoreau. Since I was interested in nature, Thoreau influenced me quite a bit. At that time, my mother had great influence on me, so when I discussed it with her, she thought it wouldn't be so good for her relations with me if I became a monk and stayed up in the woods or became a hermit. And so the next closest thing, I felt, was to become a writer, and in that she encouraged me a hundred percent. But before that, she was also my number one baseball backer-up and she used to attend all the games that I played because she thought I was pretty dedicated in baseball. In fact, for a while I was more interested in baseball than writing.

Since I was a teenager my association with my fellow Nisei as far as intellectual interests were concerned was almost nil because I found very few Nisei who would take interest in literature and art. Outside of the few students who were art students, I didn't have very many companions who would even glance at art or literature. As my main interest became literary, I had to go on my own. That more or less gave me the tendency to become a loner. I would go by myself and select my own interest, my own curiosities.

Writing during World War II

Leong: What was it like writing in the camps during the Second World War in Topaz?

Mori: Camp life was so fascinating to me because each camp had so many people (for instance, in Topaz we had eight thousand people). I used to think there were eight thousand stories to be told and each story, even by one writer, had different distinctions. Because there were so many incidents, so many different aspects, and so many backgrounds of different nature, camp life history can be retold many times from many individuals....

Leong: Do you think the Issei and Nisei had different views of the war at the time?

Mori: Well, I believe the Issei more or less felt attached to Japan simply because they were born and raised there. They remember the old Japan where they had good times as a boy or as a child and they always

Topaz Times *newspaper staff at the Topaz relocation camp. Toshio poses candidly in the first row, far left. Delta, Utah, circa 1943.*

remember Japan of that period. They didn't recognize the fact that Japan did change during the depression and became a war-like Japan—but the Issei, as a whole, remember Japan, the peaceful Japan where they had spent many wonderful years. Whereas the Nisei, as a whole, remember just early California days when they too enjoyed the California climate in spite of the discrimination.

Leong: In one story "The Long Journey and the Short Ride," you talk about your brother, and about you and your mother seeing your brother off to the European front, and your apprehension about being received outside of Topaz for the first time....

Mori: Yes, that truly happened to me. This was based on the last visit of my younger brother, who belonged to the 442nd. At that time the GIs were eligible to return and visit their families who were interned in various camps. Some of the Nisei who were already within camp used to question my brother, "How come you come back to camp where everything is denied; you're more likely to enjoy yourself outside." My brother would say that his relations with the family were deeper and he was concerned about our family and that's the reason why he returned....

237

Leong: You are really the bridge between the first generation Issei and the third generation Sansei, since you are second generation Nisei both in terms of your experience and your writing. Your son Steve is a photographer and writer himself; he's third generation.... What do you perceive as the differences among generations in their attitude toward writing and the arts and toward Asian American writers?

Mori: I believe, as a whole, and I think I'm pretty close to the actual truth, that the relationship between the Issei, the first generation, and Sansei, the third generation, is much closer. I believe that the Sansei and Yonsei have more interest in their historical background, Japanese customs and traditions. Whereas my generation, the second generation, more or less deliberately stayed away from the Japanese interest in our native Japan, especially customs, because we were trying to become pro-American, hundred-percent American citizens, and we wanted to prove to ourselves that we were loyal Americans rather than half-and-half. Because our background in California more or less made our position suspect, we studied more American things, American politics, and American traditions. Very few of us were attached even to the Issei concerns. We were so-called outcasts from Japanese knowledge by the Issei, our parents, because we would not study sincerely, although we did attend Japanese schools and all that. The Issei as a whole used to say, "*Nisei dame*," meaning "Nisei no good," because they never follow the traditions of the Japanese.

Leong: You've never been back to Japan as many of the younger second or third generation writers have. Do you have any desire to do so now?

Mori: Up to this time I have very little desire to go back and do research there, but I do have some interest there because my cousin was in Hiroshima at the time of the Hiroshima bomb. She was injured then, but she happened to fully recover and so she is still living. The reason why she was in Hiroshima city was because she was, and she still is, a bookshop owner in Otake. Incidentally, that's where my parents came from, Otake. So I do have relatives near Hiroshima who are still living. My older brother did visit there last year, and they all told me to come. I do have some desire now, but it might be a few years before I will go back, if I do.

Toshio Mori—A Brief Biography

• Late 1890's. Toshio Mori's father arrives in San Francisco. Soon after, his wife and Toshio's two older brothers join him. In San Francisco, the Mori family runs a bathhouse.

• March 3, 1910. Toshio Mori is born in Oakland, California.

• 1913–15. Mori's father sells the bathhouse, and the family moves to San Leandro to begin their own nursery.

• 1915–1930. The years of Mori's youth, in which he considers becoming a professional baseball player and a Buddhist missionary.

• 1932. At 22, Mori begins to write daily. Strongly influenced by dime novels and short-story writers such as O. Henry and Sherwood Anderson, Mori disciplines himself to write four hours each day after working a full day in his family's nursery.

• 1938. After years of rejection from mainstream American publications, Mori's story "The Brothers" is finally published in *Coast* magazine.

• 1941. December 7. Pearl Harbor is bombed, leading the United States into World War II. Subsequent anti-Japanese sentiment prompts Caxton Printers to shelve Mori's book.

• 1942. The Caxton Printers, Ltd. plans to publish Mori's collection of short stories, *Yokohama, California*.

• 1942. The Mori family is assigned to Topaz, the Central Utah Relocation Project. Toshio works as camp historian and helps create the literary journal *Trek*.

• 1943. One of Mori's short stories appears in the anthology *Best Short Stories of 1943*.

• 1945. Mori's younger brother Kazuo, who is a member of the all-Nisei 442nd Regimental Combat Team, is seriously injured on the Italian front and transferred to the veterans' hospital in Auburn, California.

• 1945. World War II ends, and Toshio Mori returns to San Leandro.

• June 29, 1947. Marries Hisayo Yoshiwara.

• 1949. *Yokohama, California* is published by Caxton Printers. The collection receives much critical acclaim and is distinguished as the first collection of short stories by a Japanese American.

• 1949–1965. Toshio Mori continues to write, and his work is regularly published in the *Pacific Citizen* and *Hokubei Mainichi*.

• July 15, 1951. Son Steven Mori born.

• 1960's. Mori Nursery closes. Mori begins working as a wholesale florist sales-man and delivery person.

• 1970's. A new generation of Sansei students, writers, and critics rediscover Mori's work, and Toshio Mori's distinction as a pioneer writer of the Asian American community is cemented.

• September 1972. Mori suffers a mild stroke, but recovers almost fully by 1973. Retires from florist business and starts lecturing at colleges and seminars as interest in his work builds.

• 1977. Asian American folk-rock group based in San Jose, California names itself "Yokohama, California" after Mori's book.

• 1978. *Woman from Hiroshima*, Mori's first novel, is published by the Isthmus Poetry Foundation.

• 1979. University of California, Los Angeles Asian American Studies Center publishes Mori's second collection of stories, *The Chauvinist and Other Stories*.

• April 12, 1980. Mori dies in his hometown, San Leandro, California.

Suggested Reading

Chan, Sucheng. *Asian Americans: An Interpretive History.* Boston: Twayne Publishers, 1991. Twayne's Immigrant Heritage of America Series. Thomas J. Archdeacon, general ed.

Daniels, Roger. *The Politics of Prejudice: The Anti-Japanese Movement in California and the Struggle for Japanese Exclusion.* 1962. 2d ed. Berkeley: University of California Press, 1977.

Higgs, Robert. "Landless by Law—Japanese Immigrants in California Agriculture to 1941." *Journal of Economic History* 38.1. (Mar. 1978).

Horokoshi, Peter. "Interview with Toshio Mori" in Gee, Emma, ed. *Counterpoint: Perspectives on Asian America.* Los Angeles: Asian American Studies Center, University of California, 1976.

Inada, Lawson Fusao. *Only What We Could Carry: The Japanese American Internment Experience.* Berkeley: Heyday Books, 2000.

Inada, Lawson Fusao. "Tribute to Toshio." In Janice Merikitani, et al., eds. *Ayumi: Japanese American Anthology.* San Francisco: Japanese American Anthology Committee, 1980.

Ito, Kazuo. *Issei: A History of Japanese Immigrants in North America.* Shinichiro Nakamura, Jean S. Gerard, trans. Seattle: Executive Committee for the publication of Issei: a History of Japanese Immigrants in North America, 1973.

Iwata, Masakazu. *Planted in Good Soil: A History of the Issei in United States Agriculture.* American University Studies, Series 9, History, vol. 57. New York: P. Lang, 1990.

Kawaguchi, Gary. *Living With Flowers, the California Flower Market History.* San Francisco: California Flower Market, Inc., 1993.

Masumoto, David Mas. *Country Voices: The Oral History of a Japanese American Family Farm Community.* Del Ray, CA: Inaka Countryside Publications, 1987.

Mayer, David R. "Akegarasu and Emerson: Kindred Spirits of Toshio Mori's 'The Seventh Street Philosopher.'" *Amerasia Journal* 16.2 (1990).

Mori, Toshio. *The Chauvinist and Other Stories.* Los Angeles: Asian American Studies Center, University of California, Los Angeles, 1979.

Mori, Toshio. *Woman from Hiroshima.* San Francisco: Isthmus Press, 1978.

Mori, Toshio. *Yokohama, California.* Introd. William Saroyan. Caldwell, ID: Caxton Printers, Ltd., 1949. Introd. Lawson Fusao Inada. Seattle: University of Washington Press, 1985.

Okada, John. *No-No Boy*. Rutland, VT: Charles E. Tuttle, 1957. San Francisco: Combined Asian American Resources Project, Inc., 1976. Seattle, University of Washington Press, 1979.

Okubo, Mine. *Citizen 13660*. New York: Columbia University Press, 1946. New York, Arno Press, 1948. Seattle, University of Washington Press, 1983.

Palumbo-Liu, David. "Toshio Mori and the Attachments of Spirit: A Response to David R. Mayer." *Amerasia Journal* 17.3 (1991).

Tateishi, John. *And Justice for All: An Oral History of the Japanese American Detention Camps*. New York: Random House, 1984.

Tsuchida, Nobuya. "Japanese Gardeners in Southern California, 1900–1942." In Cheng, Lucie, and Edna Bonacich, ed. *Labor Immigration Under Capitalism: Asian Workers in the United States Before World War II*. Berkeley: University of California Press, 1984. 435-69.

Yamamoto [DeSoto], Hisaye. *Seventeen Syllables and Other Stories*. Latham, NY: Kitchen Table Women of Color Press, 1988.

Yamauchi, Wakako. *Songs My Mother Taught Me: Stories, Plays, and Memoir*. New York: Feminist Press at the City University of New York, 1994.